Advertising Media Volume 184

FEATURE**SPOTLIGHT**

This Week in Advertising...

The VP:
Flynn Maddox

His New Campaign:
Cribs & Cradles—for the man who has it all...except the baby!

Scandal is threatening Maddox Communications yet again, and this time, Vice President Flynn Maddox is the target. According to sources, Mr. Maddox is now living with his ex-wife—who apparently was never his "ex" at all. Rumor has it that Mrs. Renee Maddox relocated from Los Angeles to the house she and Mr. Maddox shared seven years ago. But what's even more interesting is that she recently tried to gain access to her husband's sample at a sperm bank. So...what exactly is going on between husband and "ex-wife"?

Dear Reader,

Who hasn't spent time rehashing a conversation or event after the fact and come up with a much wittier response or better ending? Wouldn't it be great if life had a "do over" button?

I recently heard country song lyrics that talked about how a rock and a hard place can make a diamond. I am a firm believer that everything in life—even the bad stuff—happens for a reason, and we have lessons to learn from the events. Once we've learned those lessons we are often stronger and better equipped to deal with the next stumbling block in our path.

Executive's Pregnancy Ultimatum gave me the opportunity to grant Flynn and Renee Maddox a second chance at love when Renee's longing for a baby brings her "ex" husband back into the picture. This story also afforded me the opportunity to revisit San Francisco, one of the most romantic cities in the U.S.

I hope you enjoy the trip as much as I did.

Happy reading,

Emilie Rose

EMILIE ROSE

EXECUTIVE'S PREGNANCY ULTIMATUM

Silhouette® Desire

Published by Silhouette Books
America's Publisher of Contemporary Romance

Special thanks and acknowledgment to Emilie Rose
for her contribution to the
KINGS OF THE BOARDROOM miniseries.

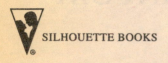 SILHOUETTE BOOKS

Recycling programs
for this product may
not exist in your area.

ISBN-13: 978-0-373-73007-0

EXECUTIVE'S PREGNANCY ULTIMATUM

Copyright © 2010 by Harlequin Books S.A.

Visit Silhouette Books at www.eHarlequin.com

Printed in U.S.A.

Books by Emilie Rose

Silhouette Desire

EMILIE ROSE

Bestselling Silhouette Desire author and RITA® Award finalist Emilie Rose lives in her native North Carolina with her four sons and two adopted mutts. Writing is her third (and hopefully her last) career. She's managed a medical office and run a home day care, neither of which offers half as much satisfaction as plotting happy endings. Her hobbies include gardening and cooking (especially cheesecake). She's a rabid country music fan because she can find an entire book in almost any song. She is currently working her way through her own "bucket list," which includes learning to ride a Harley. Visit her Web site at www.emilierose.com or e-mail EmilieRoseC@aol.com. Letters can be mailed to P.O. Box 20145, Raleigh, NC 27619.

To Cathy, Maya, Michelle, Jen and Leanne.
Ladies, it was great being part of your team.

Prologue

"**W**hat do you mean I'm still married?" Renee Maddox struggled to keep the hysteria out of her voice as she stared aghast at her attorney.

Unflappable as usual, the older gentleman sat back in his chair. "Apparently your husband never filed the papers."

"But we've been separated seven years. How could this happen?"

"Failure to file is not as uncommon as you might think, Renee. But if you want to know the real reason, then you'll have to call Flynn and ask him. Or let me do it."

The pain of failure, of love gone so horribly wrong, still hurt. She'd loved Flynn with every fiber of her being. But in the end her love hadn't been enough. "No. I don't want to call him."

"Let's look at the big picture. You're entitled to half Flynn's assets when we file again, and those assets are considerably more now than they were then."

"I'm not any more interested in Flynn's money now than I was then. I want nothing from him."

The quick flattening of her lawyer's lips told her the news didn't make him happy, and no doubt she'd hear more about the subject. "I understand that you want a quick, clean break, but remember, California is a community-property state. You could get more since you didn't have a prenuptial agreement."

Another wave of worry rippled over her. "Does that mean he could also get half of my business? I've worked too hard to make California Girl's Catering a success to give it away."

"I won't let you lose CGC. But let's revisit what brought you here today. You can change your last name regardless of your marital status."

"My name is the least of my worries right now." Her plan to take control of her life had seemed so simple, beginning with taking back her maiden name, then starting the family she'd always wanted. But Flynn had refused to...

Her thoughts skidded to a halt as an elusive memory teased her. Grasping the arms of the cool leather chair, she struggled to recall the details of the story he'd confessed over too much champagne on their honeymoon, and slowly the pieces fell into place.

Hope flickered to life inside her. She'd been aching for a baby, and when she'd turned thirty-two last month she'd decided to take matters into her own hands and quit waiting for the mythical Mr. Right to appear. Like the heroines of some of her favorite romance novels, she'd decided to get artificially inseminated via a reputable sperm bank.

She'd been reading donor profiles for weeks, but had never expected to find a donor she'd known—and once loved. She knew how many unanswered questions— some important, some not—she and her child would face down the road if she went through with her plan. She'd grown up not knowing her father's identity because her mother couldn't—or wouldn't—name the man who'd impregnated her.

"Renee, are you all right?"

"I—I'm fine." Swallowing to ease her dry mouth, Renee studied the wizened face of the man on the opposite side of the desk. "You said I'm entitled to half of everything Flynn's?"

"Yes."

Her heart raced with excitement. She struggled to regulate her quickened breaths. The idea of having Flynn's baby without his consent was ludicrous and even sneaky. It certainly wasn't the nicest thing she could do, but she desperately wanted a child, and she would never ask him for support. He'd probably forgotten about that college dare, anyway.

She wiped her damp palms on her pant legs. "While Flynn was in college he made a deposit at a sperm bank on a dare. He said he asked them to hold it 'for future use.' If the sperm bank still has his…stuff, can I have it? Or at least half of it?"

Kudos to her lawyer for not showing surprise by so much as a twitch of an eyelash. "I don't see any reason we can't pursue that option."

"Then that's what I want. I want to have Flynn's baby. And then as soon as I've conceived, I'll want a divorce."

One

February 1

The pencil snapped in Flynn's fingers Monday morning. Ledgers forgotten, he rose with the phone still pressed to his ear and walked around his desk to close his office door. He leaned against it. No one on the sixth floor of Maddox Communications needed to hear what he thought the woman on the other end of the line had just said or his reply to her statement.

"I'm sorry. Could you repeat that?"

"I'm Luisa from New Horizons Fertility Clinic. Your wife has asked to be inseminated with your sperm," a cheerful female voice enunciated precisely as if he was an idiot. At the moment he felt like one.

His *wife?* He didn't have a wife. Not anymore. A familiar hollowness settled in his chest.

"Do you mean Renee?"

"Yes, Mr. Maddox. She's asking for your sample."

Head reeling, he tried to break down this crazy conversation and make sense of it. First, why would Renee try to pass herself off as his wife when they'd been apart seven years? She'd been the one to file for divorce the minute the one-year waiting period had passed. And second, there was the donation he'd made on a stupid dare back in college. Not a wise decision. Linking the two separate incidents boggled his mind.

"My 'sample' is fourteen years old. I thought you would have disposed of it by now."

"No, sir. It's still viable. Semen, if properly stored, can last beyond fifty years. But you stipulated that your specimen not be used without your written consent. I'll need you to sign a form to release it to your wife."

She's not my wife. But he kept the rebuttal to himself. The advertising agency dealt with some extremely conservative clients. One whiff of this story getting out and they could lose business—not something Madd Comm could afford in these tight economic times.

He scanned his office—the last happy project he and his ex-wife had completed together. When he'd resigned from his previous job and joined the family advertising agency, he and Renee together had chosen the glass desk, the pair of cream leather sofas and the profusion of plants. Plants he'd managed not to kill—unlike his marriage. He and Renee had been a good team.

Had been. Past tense.

He intended to get to the bottom of this fiasco, but one thing was certain. Nobody was getting his frozen, fourteen-year-old sperm.

"Destroy the sample."

"I'll need your written consent for that, too," the faceless voice quipped back.

"Fax over the form. I'll sign it and fax it back."

"Give me your numbers and I'll get it right to you."

Flynn's mind raced as he gave the numbers by rote. He tried to recall the awful months surrounding Renee's moving out, but much of it was a blur. He'd lost his father, his architectural career and then his wife all within six miserable months. A year after Renee had moved out he'd received the divorce papers, reopening an unhealed wound. The old anger returned—anger toward Renee for giving up on them so easily and toward himself for allowing it to happen. He detested failure. None more than his own.

The fax machine in the corner beeped, signaling an incoming missive. He checked the letterhead. "It's here. I'll return it before the ink dries."

After ending the call, he whipped the sheets off the machine, read, signed and then faxed them back.

His last memory of the divorce papers was of his brother promising to mail them after they'd sat on Flynn's desk for a month because Flynn hadn't had the heart to mail them and break that final link with Renee. What had happened to the documents after Brock took them?

The back of Flynn's neck prickled. Wait a minute. He didn't remember receiving a copy of the divorce decree. Hadn't his divorced friends said something about getting an official notification in the mail?

He was divorced, wasn't he? But if so, why would Renee lie to the clinic?

Lead settled in his gut. Renee had never been a liar.

He reached for the phone to call his lawyer, but stopped. Andrew would have to track down the information and call back, and Flynn had never been good at sitting and waiting.

Brock was closer.

Flynn yanked open his door so quickly he startled his PA. "Cammie, I'll be in Brock's office."

"Do you want me to call and see if he's free?"

"No. He'll make time for this." He'd damned well better make time.

Flynn's feet pounded on the black oak floors as he strode down the hall to the opposite side of the sixth floor and Brock's west corner office. He nodded to Elle, his brother's executive assistant, but didn't slow down as he passed her desk. Ignoring her squeak of protest, he barged into Brock's office without knocking.

His brother, with the phone to his ear, looked up in surprise, then held up his finger. Flynn shook his head and made an X with his forearms in the universal "shut down" signal, then closed the door. Brock wrapped up his conversation.

"Problem?" he asked after he'd cradled the receiver.

"What did you do with my divorce papers?"

Brock jerked back in his chair. Surprise filled eyes the same blue as Flynn saw in the mirror every morning, and then the surprise turned to wariness.

Flynn's gut clenched. "You did mail them, didn't you, Brock?"

Brock rose, exhaling a slow breath. He unlocked and opened a file-cabinet drawer, then withdrew a sheaf of papers and swore under his breath. "No."

Shock rattled Flynn to the soles of his feet. "What?"

"I forgot."

His heart hammered in his chest and in his ears. "You *forgot?* How is that possible?"

Clutching the back of his neck, Brock grimaced. "I stalled initially because you were so broken up over losing Renee that I hoped once you two calmed down you'd resolve whatever issue drove you apart. I felt partially responsible for the demise of your marriage because I pressured you into leaving a career you loved to come aboard as Maddox's VP. And then I forgot. Stupid of me, but if you recall it was a tough time for all of us after Dad died."

Flynn's legs went weak. Flabbergasted, he sank into a leather chair and dropped his head in his hands.

Married. He was still married. To Renee.

A confusing swirl of responses swept through him. Tamping them down, he focused on the facts.

If Renee was passing herself off as his wife, then she must have known they weren't divorced. The question was, how long had she known, and why hadn't she called and chewed him out for not mailing the forms, or at the very least, sicced her attorney on him?

"Flynn, are you okay?"

Hell no.

"Of course," he answered automatically. He'd never been one to share his problems. He wasn't going to start now.

As his shock slowly subsided, a completely different emotion took its place. Hope. No, it was more than that. Elation filled him like helium, making him feel weightless.

He and Renee weren't divorced.

After years of silence, he had a reason to contact her. A reason besides finding out why she'd tried to pull a fast one with his sperm. But for now it was enough to know they weren't divorced and she wanted to have his baby.

The surreal feeling left him reeling. "I'll call my lawyer and find out where I stand. I'm going to take a few days off."

"You? You never take time off. But as much as I hate to say it, now is not a good time."

"I don't care. The situation has to be dealt with. Now."

"I guess you're right. Here. Again, I apologize. If you'd ever demonstrated any real interest in another woman, maybe it would have tripped my memory. Maybe not. It's a lousy excuse, but there it is. What brought on this sudden interest in your divorce? Is Renee planning to remarry?"

Flynn flinched. Logically, he knew Renee had probably dated since their separation, as had he, but the idea of her with other men filled him with a possessiveness that should have died long ago. He rose to his feet and took the document that should have ended his marriage and made an instant decision not to share the sperm news. His family was better off not knowing.

"I don't know Renee's plans. I haven't seen her in years." She'd wanted it that way. But now he would see her. His pulse accelerated at the prospect.

"Flynn, I'm sure I don't need to warn you that we need to keep this quiet, but I'm going to, anyway. News of this getting out won't help our cause against Golden Gate Promotions, and I'll be damned if I want to hear that bastard Athos Koteas crowing in glee if we lose more clients."

The mention of their rival almost dampened Flynn's excitement. "Understood."

He returned to his office and crossed straight to the shredder. Through the window above the machine, the sun glowed just above the roof lines in the distance. The symbolism of a new day and a new beginning didn't escape him. Losing Renee had been the biggest regret of his life. His older brother's negligence had given Flynn the perfect opportunity to see if the attraction was still there and if so to win her back.

He fed the papers through the slot one page at a time, enjoying the whine and grind of the machine turning his biggest failure into crosscut paper fragments. When he finished he felt like celebrating. Instead, he sat down at his computer.

He needed to locate his wife.

MADCOM2.

The light blue BMW's license plate snagged Renee's attention as she turned into her driveway. She almost clipped her mailbox post with her minivan's front bumper and quickly jerked the wheel to the left.

MADCOM equaled Maddox Communications.

Her stomach churned like a dough mixer as she parked beside her visitor. She knew the identity of the car's owner from the "2" part of the tag before her ex— her *husband*—climbed from the driver's seat.

Ever since she'd heard the clinic's message on her answering machine informing her that her request for Flynn's sperm had been denied, she'd known it was only a matter of time before he came looking for her. The clinic must have contacted him. Her attorney had warned her of the possibility.

But nothing could prepare her for Flynn looming over her car even before she could pull the key from the ignition. The moment she disengaged the locks, he opened her door. Heart racing and her mouth going dry, she fought to appear calm, grabbed her purse from the passenger seat and stepped from the vehicle, ignoring the hand he offered in assistance. She couldn't touch him yet, and wasn't sure she'd ever be ready for that again even in the most casual way.

Dreading the conversation ahead, she tipped back her head to look up at the man she'd once loved with all her heart. The man who'd broken her.

Flynn had changed. And yet he hadn't. His eyes were still impossibly blue and his hair inky dark, but a few strands of silver now glimmered at his temples. His shoulders were as broad as she remembered and even with him wearing his suit, she could tell he hadn't added any fat to his lean torso. If anything, his jaw looked more chiseled.

But the past seven years had been hard on him. There were grooves beside the mouth she'd once lived to kiss, and a new horizontal crease divided his brow. She didn't think those were laugh lines fanning out from his eyes, although he used to smile often during the early days of their relationship, before he'd begun to work for Maddox Communications.

"Hello, Flynn."

"Renee. Or should I say, wife?" His deep, gravelly tone filled her tummy with the sensation of scattering butterflies. "How long have you known?"

She could have played dumb, but didn't see the point. "That we weren't divorced? Only a few weeks."

"And you didn't call me."

"Like you didn't call me when you decided not to file the papers?"

He frowned at her snippy tone. "There's more to it than that."

"Enlighten me." And then she remembered the

Wednesday-morning fish-market cargo in her cooler. "But you'll have to finish this riveting story inside. I have to get the seafood into the fridge."

She opened the van's back door. His hip and shoulder bumped hers when he nudged her aside to grab the cooler. Her senses went wild over the contact. The way they used to. Darn it. Her reaction didn't mean anything. She was over him. Well and truly over him. He'd ripped out her heart piece by piece before she'd left him. No feelings remained other than regret and disappointment.

"Get the door," he ordered.

His words shocked her into motion. She locked the car and hustled up the flower-lined brick sidewalk of her bungalow, scanning the exterior and trying to see it through Flynn's eyes. He hadn't been here since the early days of their short marriage when this had been her grandmother's home. Renee had made a lot of changes since then as she'd turned a private retreat into an inviting place of business.

She'd added flower beds beneath the lemon and orange trees, as well as a bubbling fountain, and she'd hung multiple trailing-flower baskets and a swing on the porch. The stone foundation and shingled exterior had been pressure-washed last year and the trim freshly painted a rich emerald-green, but she'd done the majority of her work inside.

She unlocked and pushed open the front door, then followed him through the foyer and living room to the kitchen, her masterpiece.

He stopped abruptly. "You've expanded."

"I needed a larger kitchen for my catering business, so I enclosed Grandma's back porch and redid everything. I'm using her old bedroom for an office."

Stop babbling.

She closed her mouth and focused on her stainless, commercial-grade appliances, acres of granite counter-tops and bright white cabinet—a cook's dream. Her dream. Something she had not been allowed to pursue as Flynn's wife.

"Nice. What made you decide to open your own business?"

"It was something I'd always wanted. Granny talked me into taking the leap before she passed away four years ago."

From the shock in his eyes, she guessed he hadn't known about her grandmother's passing. She probably should have notified him, but she'd had enough heart-ache to deal with over losing Granny without having to face Flynn at the funeral.

"I'm sorry for your loss. Emma was a wonderful lady."

"Yes, she was. I don't know what I would have done without her, and I still miss her. But she would have loved this—another generation of Landers women working with food and feeding the masses."

"I'm sure she would."

In the silence that followed, Renee looked across the kitchen to the ladder-back chair that had been her granny's favorite. There were days when it felt as if Emma were watching over her, but then, Emma had been more of a mother to Renee than her own had been. Her grandmother had certainly been a rock of support when Renee had arrived brokenhearted on her doorstep after leaving Flynn. Emma had opened her arms, her heart and her home, offering Renee a sanctuary for as long as she needed one.

"Where do you want the cooler?" Flynn asked.

"On the floor in front of the fridge." As soon as he

set it down, she transferred twenty pounds of shrimp and six large salmon filets into her Sub-Zero refrigerator, then washed her hands and faced him. "So…what's so complicated about slapping a stamp on the envelope containing the divorce paperwork?"

"Brock thought he was doing us a favor by giving us cool-down time. He put the papers in a file cabinet."

"For six years?"

"They'd probably still be in the drawer if you hadn't tried to get my sperm." Eyes narrowing, he leaned against the counter and crossed his arms and ankles. "So you still want to have my baby."

His speculative tone put her on guard. "I want to have *a* baby. You just happened to be a donor I knew."

"And you planned to have my child without informing me?"

She grimaced. "Probably not one of my best decisions. But after going through page after page of other potential donors, I had too many unanswered questions. But now that you've refused I'll go back to my anonymous candidates."

His unblinking gaze held hers. "Not necessarily."

"What do you mean?"

"Renee, I always wanted you to have my baby."

"Not true. I asked seven and a half years ago. Correction, I begged. You said no."

"The timing was wrong. I was trying to adjust to my new job."

"A job you hated. One that made you miserable."

"Brock and Maddox Communications needed me."

"So did I, Flynn." She hated the telling crack in her voice, but the sadness of watching their love unravel hit her all over again, making her throat tighten. "I needed the man I fell in love with, the one I married. I was more than willing to help you deal with your grief over losing your father. But I couldn't stand by and watch that job destroy you. You gave up your dream of becoming an architect and in the process became a silent, uncommunicative stranger. We didn't talk. We didn't make love. You were barely ever home."

"I was working, not cheating on you."

"Watching our love die was more than I could bear."

"When did it die?"

"You tell me." When she'd caught herself turning to alcohol to dull the pain of her unhappiness, she'd known that no matter how much she loved him she'd end up just like her bitter, unhappy alcoholic mother if she didn't get out. If she'd stayed, Flynn would have ended up hating her the way each of her mother's lovers had eventually despised her mother over the years.

The childhood memories of loud arguments, slamming doors, cars roaring off and "uncles" who never returned had been too vivid. She couldn't live that way and she would never raise a child in that atmosphere.

"I loved you right up until the day you left me. We could have made it work, Renee, if you'd given us a chance."

"I don't think so. Not as long as you had a job that sucked the life out of you. Out of us." She tried to shake off the bad memories. "I'll have my attorney draw up another set of divorce papers. Like last time, I want nothing from you."

"Except my child."

Another dream dead. They'd once planned to have a large family—at least three children, maybe four, because she'd hated being an only child. "Like I said, I'll go back to my donors."

"You don't have to."

Her heartbeat blipped out of rhythm. "What are you saying?"

"You can have my baby."

She forced a breath into her tight chest. "The clinic said your sample had been destroyed. Are you planning to make another donation?"

"I'm not talking about frozen sperm or artificial insemination."

Her tongue felt as dry as parchment paper. "Then what are you suggesting, Flynn?"

"I'll give you my baby—the usual way."

Stunned by the idea of making love with Flynn again, she staggered backward into the counter. But an undeniable wisp of desire snaked through her. They'd been so good together. She'd experienced nothing remotely close to that level of fulfillment before or since Flynn. But she couldn't risk it.

"No. That isn't an option. I didn't do casual sex before and I'm not going to start now."

"It's not casual sex when we're still married. I know how much not knowing anything about your father bothered you. This way you'll know who fathered your child, and you'll have my complete medical history."

Tempting. And dangerous. "Why would you agree to that?"

"I'm thirty-five. It's time to think about kids."

Alarm ripped through her. "I'm not looking for someone to be a part of my child's life."

"Your catering business takes up what? Fifty, sixty hours a week? When are you going to have time to be a parent?"

Had he been checking up on her? "I'll make time."

"Like Lorraine did?"

She winced as the barb hit deep. "That's low—even for you, Flynn."

Her mother had worked long hours as a chef in a series of swanky L.A. restaurants and would then come home to drink until she passed out. Typical of a functional alcoholic, only her family had suffered. Her mother had hidden her addiction well from her employers and the rest of the world.

"It will be easier to raise a child with two parents and better for the child. It's also a good backup plan in case something happens to either of us."

Horrified by his implication, she backed away. "We might still be married, but we're not staying that way."

"I want to share every aspect of the pregnancy and delivery and be a part of the baby's first year. After that we can go our separate ways—other than sharing custody. We'll keep the option open for our child to have the siblings you never had."

"More children? Are you crazy?" But what he said appealed on so many levels. Too many levels.

"I want to be a father, Renee. I want a family."

"Don't you have a girlfriend or someone your mother would approve of who could—"

"I could ask you the same question. No men in the picture?"

"I'm not seeing anyone." She'd be insane to risk her heart and her health again. Shaking her head, she paced to the opposite side of the kitchen. "Thanks for your generous offer, but I'll stick with my donor catalog."

"You'd rather depend on a questionnaire that's probably no more truthful than a personal ad?"

Another direct hit. She had wondered how factual the

donor data might be. Sure, the lab results would be accurate, but she'd done enough online dating in the past few years to know that answers applicants provided rarely resembled the truth. "I'll choose carefully."

"Think about it, Renee. The plans we made. The house we bought and restored together specifically with raising a family in mind. The fenced yard. The dog. The whole deal. Your baby could have all that."

Her heart squeezed. "You still have the house?"

"Yes."

They'd spent the first six months of their marriage working side by side renovating the beautiful Victorian in Pacific Heights. She'd spent the second six months wandering around the empty rooms alone trying to figure out how to save her dying marriage. In the end, all she could do was save herself.

"Flynn, it's a crazy idea."

"So was us running away to Vegas to get married. But it worked."

"For a while. And judging by your license plate, you still work for Maddox Communications. Nothing has changed."

"The job is under control now. It doesn't consume me like it used to. Move in with me. Let's make a baby, Renee."

She gaped at him. "Move in with you? What about my business? I've spent years building California Girl's Catering. I can't walk away for a year and expect my clientele to be waiting when I come back. And I can't commute. It's a five- or six-hour drive each way without traffic."

"I checked out your Web page. You have 'an amazingly talented assistant' who helps you, or so you claim on your blog. Leave the L.A. business in her hands temporarily and expand into the San Francisco area. I have connections. I'll help you."

He certainly knew which buttons to push to get her acquiescence. She didn't doubt for one second that Tamara could handle the L.A. side of the business, and having the Maddox clout behind CGC would certainly get her foot in the door of the highly competitive San Francisco marketplace faster.

But were the risks worth the potential rewards?

"Have my child. Allow me to spend the baby's first year under the same roof, and then I'll give you an uncontested divorce and pay full child support."

A tiny, sentimental part of her wanted to agree. Renee had always believed Flynn would make a wonderful father—the kind she wished she'd had. She'd experienced firsthand how patient and encouraging he could be when he'd taught her the skills of restoration. But letting him back into her life was scary and risky.

You're older, wiser and stronger now. You can handle it.

She had to be crazy, because she was actually considering his suggestion. But maybe…just maybe this insane idea could work. Focus on the result. A baby. Someone to love and come home to each night. But if she was going to keep her head and her sanity, she needed to lay ground rules.

"Flynn, hooking up just to have a baby is crazy."

"It could work—for both of us."

"If I agree to this, then I'll need help finding kitchen space in San Francisco."

"I'll get right on it."

She rubbed her cold hands together. Her heart

pounded wildly out of rhythm. She gulped, trying to ease the knot in her throat. "Okay, I'll consider it, but I have a few conditions."

Victory flared in his eyes, giving her a moment's panic. "Name them."

"We need time to get to know each other again and make sure this crazy scheme can work before jumping back into bed together."

"How much time?"

"I don't know. A month, I guess. That should be long enough to determine whether or not we're still compatible."

"Agreed."

"If it's not working, then either of us can back out and you will sign the divorce papers."

He dipped his chin. "I'll sign."

The sense of panic squeezed tighter, as if she was drowning and desperate for air. Was she crazy to plan on bringing a baby into a broken marriage? But she and Flynn had never had the kind of volatile arguments her mother and her mother's lovers had had. Their child would not feel like a bone of contention. Her baby would know from day one that it was wanted, planned, not a mistake that derailed her life.

"I—I want my own bedroom. We'll get together… when it's time…*if* we decide to go through with the plan."

The crease in his forehead deepened. "If you insist."

"I do." She smothered a wince at the words she'd spoken so many years ago. Back then her heart and head had been filled with happiness, dreams and possibilities, instead of a stomach-twisting fear that she was making a huge mistake.

"Anything else?"

She searched her brain for more protective barriers to build, but her thoughts churned so chaotically she could barely think. "Not at the moment. But I reserve the right to revisit this later, if need be."

"I accept your terms and have a few of my own."

She stiffened. "Let's hear them."

"I want to keep the real reason for our living together between us. It is critical that our family, friends and business associates believe we are trying to reconcile rather than temporarily hook up to make a baby."

Could she fake that kind of happiness? For a baby she could do almost anything. "I guess that would be better in the long run—especially if there is a child."

"Then we have a deal?"

Doubts swirled through her like fruit pureeing in a blender.

Think of the baby. A beautiful blue-eyed, black-haired, chubby-cheeked baby.

She nodded and extended her hand. Flynn's long fingers encircled hers. He simultaneously tugged and stepped forward, then covered her mouth with his.

Shock crashed over her like a waterfall as his warm, firm lips moved against hers. Familiar sensations deluged her, sweeping her back into a current of desire and far out of her depth. Even though he was six feet and she was barely five foot three, they'd always fit together like perfectly cut puzzle pieces. His thigh spliced between hers, his strong arms enfolded her, tucking her into his chest. It felt as if she'd never left his arms, and she was right back where she was supposed to be.

Horrified, she broke the kiss and shoved against his chest. Gasping for air, she backed away, but she couldn't deny the turbulent flood of hunger sluicing through her. "What was that about?"

"Sealing the deal."

"Don't do it again."

"I'm not allowed to touch you?"

"No. Not until…it's time."

"Renee, to make our reconciliation look real, we're going to have to touch and kiss and act like we're in love."

"I'm a caterer, not an actress."

He dragged a knuckle down her cheek and over the pulse hammering in her neck, then along the neckline of her top. She shivered and her nipples tightened.

"Let your body do the talking. You still want me and it shows."

She gasped at his audacity. Unfortunately, he told the truth. Her reaction to a simple kiss told her she still wanted her husband. And wanting Flynn was the worst possible thing that could happen.

If she wasn't careful, Flynn Maddox would break her heart all over again or worse, drive her to self-destruction. And then she'd be no good for anyone—especially her child.

Two

There's no place like home.

But this wasn't her home, no matter how it felt, Renee reminded herself Friday evening. A knot of apprehension formed in her stomach as she stared up at the tall, Queen Anne Victorian house painted brick-red with cream-colored balusters and gingerbread trim.

The wooden front door with its oval, beveled-glass insert opened and Flynn stepped onto the porch. He must have been watching for her. In faded jeans and a blue T-shirt, he looked so much like the man she'd fallen in love with eight and half years ago that it felt as if someone had dropped a fifty-pound bag of sugar on her chest.

But that love had died. Painfully. And it wasn't coming back. She wouldn't let it.

A volatile cocktail of emotions churned inside her as he jogged down the steep stairs toward her, then stopped on the concrete driveway a foot away. "I'll take these bags. You grab the rest of your stuff."

Her gaze dropped briefly and involuntarily to his lips before she ripped it away. "This is all I brought."

She'd only brought the minimal requirements. She was only a visitor here, and she didn't want Flynn—or herself—to get the wrong idea that this was anything more than a temporary residence. "I'll pick up anything else I need when I make my weekly visits to check on Tamara and CGC."

He didn't look pleased, but he didn't argue. "Would you like to park your car in the garage?"

"No, thanks. Did you ever do anything with the rest of the basement?" They'd been debating what to do with the large space behind the garage after he finished using it for a workroom during renovations. Since the area was on the downhill side of the house and had plenty of windows overlooking the back garden, the empty space would be wasted as a storage room.

"Not yet, but I have some ideas."

She scanned the exterior of the house, loving every line of the gingerbread trim and dental moldings, the steep roof and the round turret. "It doesn't look like you've made any changes to the exterior."

"It's hard to improve on perfection. We did well with Bella."

Bella. The pet name they'd given the beautiful house.

Flynn's fingers covered hers on the handles of her suitcases, sending sparks shooting up her arm. He stood too close and he smelled too good and too familiar. Memories of happier times pushed their way forward. She battled them back, released her luggage and moved a safer distance away.

He carried her luggage up the steps as if the heavy bags weighed nothing. She followed him but paused on the porch to turn and look at the view. Other restored nineteenth-century Victorians lined the east-west ridge like a brightly painted rainbow of color. On days like today when the sky was clear, she could see the Golden Gate Bridge, Alcatraz and the Marin Headlands to the north. The shopping and dining districts were down the steep hill and around the block.

"Come in, Renee."

Dread slowed her reaction time. Turning her back on the gorgeous view that made real estate in the area so expensive, she stepped into the foyer. Nostalgia washed over her. She could have walked out just yesterday, instead of an aeon ago. The warm, rich, jewel-tone colors they'd chosen welcomed her exactly as she remembered. Even the scent of the vanilla and cinnamon potpourri she'd loved lingered.

Gleaming hardwood floors stretched in every direction. The staircase with its delicately carved ivory-painted spindles rose up the side wall from the center of the foyer. The formal parlor took up the front left corner of the first floor and the dining area the right.

She pulled her thoughts back to the present. "Have you finished the third floor yet?"

"There didn't seem to be much point."

Their children's rooms would have been on the third floor. Three bedrooms and a playroom.

"You can't quit, Flynn. Bella deserves to be finished."

"Now that you're back, maybe we'll get around to it."

We'll. She rejected the word.

The house had been a wreck when Flynn bought it ten years ago. He'd been restoring the first floor when they met in a local paint store where she'd driven just to find a specific brand of unscented paint that the L.A. stores hadn't carried. He'd asked her opinion on an exterior color, and the rest, as the cliché said, was history.

They'd spent many of their dates and the first six months of their marriage finishing the first floor and then the second. They'd been about to tackle the third when he'd lost his father and changed jobs, and renovations had ceased to matter to him. Just like their marriage and her. She'd continued working on the house, but it hadn't been the same. Without Flynn by her side, her heart hadn't been in the project, and when he'd refused to have a baby, there had been no point in finishing the nursery.

He climbed the stairs. "You have your choice of bedrooms—the guest room or the master."

And sleep with the memories of making love with him in that big bed and in the master bath's claw-foot tub? No, thanks. They had eventually "christened" every room in the house, so there were literally memories to suppress every way she turned, but she still wanted to be as far away from Flynn as possible.

"I'll take the front room with the balcony." The one where they'd made love on a paint-spattered drop cloth. She'd found paint in her hair and other interesting places for weeks afterward. But that day and the drop cloth were long gone.

He frowned. "Are you sure? The guest room's on the street side."

"One of us has to sleep there, and it's not like you have a lot of traffic noise here. I always thought the balcony would be a great place for guests to sit and sip coffee in the morning. You have to admit the view is incredible."

He carried her luggage into the guest quarters and set it on the iron bed. "You know where everything is. Help yourself."

"Thank you," she said as stiffly as if she was a stranger, instead of the one who'd chosen the decor of this room—right down to the wedding-ring quilt on the bed and the rug beneath her feet.

"When you're finished unpacking we'll have dinner at Gianelli's."

Memories of the quaint Italian restaurant lambasted her. "Don't even think of trying to act like everything is the same, Flynn. It isn't."

"Those who know us will expect us to celebrate our reconciliation at our favorite restaurant."

Unfortunately, Flynn was right. To make this look real she was going to have to face the demons from her past.

"Our *pretend* reconciliation," she corrected.

He inclined his head.

Resignation settled over her like a cold, wet table-cloth. The charade was going to force her into places she didn't want to go.

"Give me thirty minutes." Maybe by then she'd find the courage to do what she had to do.

Flynn loved a good plan and thus far his was coming together nicely. Renee was home. She wasn't in his bed yet. But she would be. Soon.

He laced his fingers through hers as they strolled to Gianelli's the way they'd done so many times before. She startled and tried to pull away, stumbling over an expansion joint in the sidewalk in the process. He tightened his grip, halting her fall and pulling her closer to his side.

Her wide, blue-violet eyes found his. "What are you doing?"

"Holding your hand. You can tolerate that for appearances' sake, can't you?" Having her close felt good.

"I guess so."

He inhaled, letting her familiar Gucci Envy Me perfume wash over him. He wanted to tangle his hands in her long, blond curls and kiss her until she melted against him like she used to, but that would have to wait until she was more receptive. The initial kiss had answered his primary question. The chemistry between them hadn't faded, and as long as they had chemistry to work with, he had a good chance of fixing what he'd broken.

He could feel Renee's tension through her fingers and sought a way to distract her. "I've done some research on available properties in the area for you to lease."

Her beautiful, blue-violet gaze flickered his way. "And?"

"There are a few prospects, but everything depends on your budget. I'll show you the data when we get back, along with my ideas for the basement."

Genuine interest brightened her face. "What did you decide to do with it?"

"That will have to wait until we get home."

"Tease," she said with a smile that faded almost instantly.

She no doubt remembered the occasions when she'd used the same word in the past—times when he'd aroused the hell out of her but delayed her pleasure repeatedly until she'd begged for mercy.

His skin flushed with heat and his groin grew heavy. He focused on what he planned to show her after dinner.

Drawing the blueprints for her business had filled him with an energy and excitement he hadn't experienced in a long time. He'd wanted to share them with her earlier when she'd asked about the space. But first he needed to ply her with good food, good wine and good memories to make her more receptive.

He opened the restaurant's heavy wooden door, and Mama Gianelli, thanks to a heads-up text from him, waited by the hostess stand. The women had bonded years ago when Renee had asked the restaurant owner's advice on a recipe.

Mama Gianelli squealed and bustled forward to hug Renee and kiss her cheeks. "When Flynn asked me to reserve your table, my heart overflowed. It makes me so happy to have you back where you belong, Renee. I've missed you and that beautiful smile," she gushed in her heavily accented English.

Renee's smile made its first appearance since she'd come back into his life. Too bad it wasn't aimed at him, because like Senora Gianelli, he'd missed it and the way it made Renee's eyes sparkle. "I've missed you, too, Mama G."

"And this one." Mama G pointed at Flynn and he stiffened. "He has not been eating like he should. Look at him. Skin and bones."

Flynn shifted uncomfortably, then Renee's gaze coasted over him, slowly, thoroughly. The appreciation he saw in her eyes made him stiffen for an entirely different reason.

Mama G linked her arm through Renee's. "Come, I have your special table ready."

He followed the women to the back corner, taking the time to admire his wife's petite shape from behind.

Renee had gained a little weight since their split, but it had landed in all the right places, and her white wrap-around sweater and gray trousers that accentuated her figure awakened his libido in a way no other woman had been able to do since Renee had left him.

"I will bring a bottle of your favorite Chianti to the table," their hostess said.

Renee shook her head. "None for me, thanks."

Surprised, he studied her face, but he could roll with her decision. "I'll pass, as well."

Mama Gianelli departed and Renee opened her menu. He didn't know why she was wasting her time unless hiding behind the menu was her way of avoiding him. She'd ordered the same dish each time they'd eaten here in the past, claiming no one made spinach manicotti as well.

"Aren't you ordering your usual?"

"I want to try the chicken romano. It's stuffed with shrimp and fresh mozzarella and covered in a lemon cream sauce," she replied without looking at him.

"That's a change."

She peered at him over the menu, her gaze serious. "I've changed, Flynn. I'm not the quiet little mouse who's eager to please and afraid to make waves anymore."

Was there a warning in her tone? "Everybody changes, Renee, but the fundamentals that make us who we are remain the same."

The Gianellis' granddaughter arrived to take their order. After she left, Flynn lifted his water glass. "To us and our future family."

Renee hesitated, then raised hers. "To the baby we might make."

He noted the way she stressed "might," but let it

pass, and reached across the table to capture her free hand. She stiffened. "Is this really necessary?"

"We always held hands while we waited for our food in the past."

Her fingers remained stiff in his. "Why is it so important that everyone believe we're a happy couple?"

Not the relaxing conversation he'd planned, but she needed to know the facts. He stroked his thumb across her palm. "The tight economy is pinching advertising budgets for even the largest firms. Our closest rival, Golden Gate Promotions, is encroaching on our turf and not above using underhanded methods to steal our accounts."

"For example?"

"Athos Koteas, the owner, will do anything to make us look unstable, immoral or untrustworthy."

"How can he do that?"

"Gossip. Innuendo. We don't know where he's getting his information, but it's almost as if he has an inside source. Some of our biggest clients are ultraconservative. They'll go elsewhere at the first hint of scandal because they can't afford to have their names attached to anyone who might cause them to lose customers and revenue. That's why the truth behind our personal project needs to be kept confidential."

"That's like living in a glass house, Flynn. You can't keep it up indefinitely."

"Koteas is seventy. He won't live forever. But enough about my work."

"I like hearing about your work. You never used to discuss it…well, not after you joined Maddox."

"I had enough of the advertising jungle during the day. I didn't want to rehash it at night." But she had a point. When he'd been at Adams Architecture he'd been so excited about his work that he'd often recounted the highlights of his day over dinner. "How is Lorraine?"

Her stern expression told him she'd recognized his change of topic, but then she shrugged. "Mom's the same. She's working at a five-star restaurant in Boca Raton now."

"Does she still change jobs every few years?"

Renee nodded. "She moves on as soon as someone gets on her bad side."

"That's the negative side of her alcoholism. You're very lucky to have had your grandmother to provide a more stable environment." He scraped his thumbnail across her palm. Her breath hitched. She yanked her hand free and reached for her water—but he didn't miss the goose bumps on her arms.

"You look good, Renee. Owning your own business must suit you."

"Thanks. There are advantages to being the boss, and I admit, I prefer having the freedom to be creative, instead of always being stuck with the tried-and-true recipes."

When they'd met she'd been employed by a well-known L.A. caterer. After they'd married she'd quit her job and moved to San Francisco.

He'd had a lot of time to think about the demise of their marriage, and he'd concluded his first mistake had been in asking Renee to focus full-time on their marriage and home. Much to his mother's disgust, Renee had come from a working-class family. Her grandmother had owned and run a trendy diner, and then Renee's mother had become a top chef. Both jobs required long hours, exhausting work and a willingness to get their hands dirty.

Renee was no stranger to hard work. She'd practically been raised in a bustling restaurant kitchen. At fourteen when he'd been building models and acting like a typical teenager, she'd been busing tables at her first job. She'd been accustomed to earning her own money and had never been comfortable coming to him for cash to buy groceries or anything else.

Lunch and shopping expeditions, unless related to home improvement, had never excited her, and she wasn't the type to laze in the spa. Being a lady of leisure hadn't come easily to her, and she'd had nothing to distract her when his hours increased.

Nothing except premature ideas about a baby.

He'd asked himself a hundred times if they would still be married if he'd let her take another job or if he'd said yes to the baby. But he'd refused to start a family because he hadn't wanted to be the absentee father his had been.

Children. How many would they have had by now if he hadn't said no? He brushed the thought aside. The past couldn't be undone. The only thing he could do was learn from his mistakes and move on. And this time, he didn't intend to let her go.

It would be far too easy to forget this reconciliation wasn't real, Renee decided as Flynn let her into the front door of their—his house.

During dinner he had been attentive, witty and conversational—just as he'd been during the beginning of their relationship. But he'd changed once and he could again, she reminded herself. Besides, he wasn't the real problem. She was.

"I have a set of keys for you," he said so close to her ear that his breath stirred her hair.

Awareness shivered over her. Uh-oh. She put a yard

of space between them in the foyer. "You said you'd show me your ideas for the basement."

"They're in my study, along with the keys. Go on in. I'll join you in a moment." He headed toward the kitchen.

Renee wandered down the hall to the room tucked beneath the stairs. Flynn's office smelled like him. She caught herself inhaling deeply and stopped. His drafting table still took up most of the space beneath the bay window. She was surprised he hadn't gotten rid of it since it represented the life and the dream he'd abandoned.

It seemed such a waste that he'd thrown away four years of college and four and a half more of his internship. He'd been so close to getting his credentials and ready to fulfill his dream of designing homes. Saddened, she let her eyes skim over the architectural texts and titles still occupying his floor-to-ceiling shelves, then they skidded to a halt on the framed photograph taken on their wedding day.

Melancholy thickened her throat, trapping her breath in her chest. She and Flynn looked so happy standing in front of the little white Vegas wedding chapel with their blinding smiles and love-filled eyes. But that had been before the threads of their marriage had begun unraveling, before his mother's confidence-eroding attacks had started hitting their mark and before his father had died.

In that blissfully ignorant moment frozen in the photo, Renee hadn't had a clue how silent and lonely being married to the man she loved could be. Or how weak she could become. Discovering she had feet of clay had not been one of her better moments.

A pop startled her into spinning around. Flynn entered the room carrying a bottle of wine. He had two glasses pressed against his body in the crook of his arm.

She held up a hand. "None for me."

His brow pleated. He set the bottle and glasses on a side table. His strong hands worked the cork free from the corkscrew. "Dr. Loosen used to be your favorite Riesling."

"I don't drink anymore unless I have to sample something for work. Even then, I sip and spit."

"You used to love wine."

She shrugged. "That was then."

"Did you quit because of your mother?"

He didn't know about the morning Renee had woken up on the sofa after drinking herself into oblivion while waiting for him to come home. And he never would. "Partly. The basement?"

"In a minute." He recorked the wine and, still frowning, settled behind his desk. He opened a drawer, withdrew a key ring and offered it to her. She remained frozen in place. Taking that set of keys would be another giant step forward, a blind leap over the edge of a cliff. Gathering her will, she took them from him. The cold metal bit into her hand as she closed her fist.

Next he opened a file folder and then slid it across the desk in her direction. "These are the nearby available properties that could be made to suit a catering company."

She leaned forward and scanned the first page, gasping at the numbers, then she turned to the second. He'd taken the time to list the pros and cons of each property along the margin in his familiar script. Heart sinking, she continued turning and skimming pages. Each one had high monthly rents she didn't even want to contemplate for a new business and renovation requirements that staggered her. She glanced up at Flynn and found his narrowed eyes focused on her face.

"None of the leases includes the improvements you'd

have to make to get the building up to code for California Girl's Catering. Since you've recently done that type of work, you know better than I what kind of expenses you'd incur."

Mind racing, she ticked through possibilities. Even if she used her emergency money, she didn't have the kind of cash a project of this size required. She'd have to get a loan.

Did she really want to go into debt for something that might not pan out? The San Francisco market was notoriously tough. Borrowing a large sum would also leave her trapped in San Francisco if this bargain of theirs went sour and she wanted out in a hurry. She wanted to kick herself for not checking into the costs before agreeing to Flynn's bargain.

"I don't have that kind of budget," she admitted.

"There is another less expensive option." He rose and crossed to his drafting table.

Her pulse quickened as he flipped over a large sheet of blueprint paper revealing a page covered in sketches. "You've drawn up plans."

His gaze met hers, and for the first time in ages the fire of excitement that had initially drawn her to him in that paint store gleamed in the blue depths of his eyes. "Take a look."

A little leery of her body's breathless reaction to a glimpse of the old Flynn, she edged closer. He'd sketched out a kitchen very similar to hers back in L.A., only this space was larger and had more work surfaces and bigger windows in one corner. The layout also included an office area where she could work or meet with clients and an outside patio complete with tables and a fountain.

"This is beautiful, Flynn. Where is it?"

"Our basement."

Alarm sirens screeched in her head. "But—"

He held up one broad palm. "Hear me out. The basement is a rent-free space with a separate entrance. You could work downstairs and have a nanny keep the baby upstairs. You'd be able to slip away to visit our child whenever you wanted."

Our basement. *Our* child. *Her* panic.

Her stomach fell faster than a soufflé. The words implied a long-term commitment—one she wasn't prepared to make. "Investing that much money into a temporary workplace is not a good idea, Flynn."

"Who says it has to be temporary?"

Panic prickled through her anew. "I do. Even if the San Francisco branch succeeds and I decide to keep it, I'll have this baby and then I'll hire a manager and move back to L.A. We agreed to divorce after the baby's first year."

"Think about it, Renee. You won't find a better location or price than this one. It's a trendy address with the right demographics, and it's close enough to the dining and shopping district to make it convenient and easy for clients to find."

Not only was he right, he'd literally and figuratively drawn a tempting, almost irresistible picture.

She wanted to refuse, but she'd go crazy living in San Francisco with nothing to do but wait for the sound of his car turning into the driveway. Having failed at that life already, she didn't dare risk it again—not even for a baby. Living vicariously through him and his job wasn't enough. She needed her own interests and her own financial security.

She had to work, and working for another caterer

wouldn't allow her the freedom to help Tamara in L.A. when the need arose. Not to mention, it would be a conflict of interest. It was unlikely anyone would want to risk her stealing their ideas for her own company.

Unfortunately, what Flynn proposed was both the best and worst option out there, and opening CGC in his Victorian might be the only way she could make expanding into the competitive San Francisco market a financially feasible option.

But did she really want to eat, sleep and work in Flynn's shadow? Setting up shop in his basement while living in his house would mean exactly that. Was she strong enough to handle that kind of pressure? Last time she'd crumbled under the stress.

For sanity's sake, housing CGC here would have to be a temporary solution, and if this branch succeeded she would find an alternative property as soon as she had an idea of her income and budget. That way she'd be nearby whenever her child visited his father, and her baby would never feel as if Mom couldn't wait to get him out of her hair.

You can do this. You're strong. You won't drink, whine or bemoan how the world is against you. Your son or daughter will know from day one that it is wanted, planned, not a mistake that derailed your life.

You are not your mother.

She looked down at the data Flynn had spread before her and then back at him. "It's not that I don't trust your research, but I've learned to do things for myself. I'll check around and get back to you."

Three

Flynn hadn't lied.

With a mug of coffee in hand and a sense of doom weighing heavily on her shoulders, Renee stood in the cool basement Sunday morning studying the empty, unfinished space. Flynn's plans lay on the nearby worktable for reference.

She'd spent all day Saturday looking at properties with a real estate agent only to reinforce Flynn's findings. But then, she'd always been able to trust Flynn. *She* was the one she had to worry about.

Property in the area was out of her price range unless she took on more debt than she wanted or leased space in an area where she wouldn't feel safe coming and going alone early in the morning or late at night.

She credited her grandmother for her frugal nature. Even after Granny had earned a large sum by selling her

onde and thin to the point of emaciation, Carol
ged to show disapproval despite her stiff, overly
xed face. "So it's true. You're back."

Yes." One single word shouldn't provide so much
sfaction, but given the number of times Flynn's
ther had deliberately made her miserable, Renee
k great pleasure in knowing she'd ruined Carol's
y—probably her entire week.

Carol's condemning gaze ran over Renee, from her
angled morning hair and unmade-up face, to her jeans
and department-store polo shirt to her bare feet with un-
painted toenails, then returned to her mug. "I'd like a cup
of coffee. That is, if you've learned to brew a decent pot."

Renee's temper rose, but she bit her tongue rather
than stoop to Carol's level. "Come in, but if you're ex-
pecting Kopi Luwak you'll be disappointed," she said,
naming the most expensive coffee in the world.

She led the way to the kitchen rather than the parlor,
where she had entertained her mother-in-law in the past.
Without ceremony, she filled a sturdy mug, instead of
the good china, and brought it, the sugar and the milk
carton to the table.

In business, presentation was everything. But with
Carol there was no point trying to impress her. No
matter what Renee did it was never good enough. A
lesson Renee had learned the hard way.

Carol made a production out of preparing her coffee,
then sipped and grimaced. She set the mug down. "What
game are you playing by coming back into Flynn's life
when he finally has someone he cares deeply for and
who suits him?"

Dismay and denial rippled through Renee in quick
succession, surprising her. But the acid burn in her belly

secret oatmeal cookie recipe to a national company,
she'd kept the diner and lived within her means. Granny's only luxury had been the bungalow she'd bought
with a fraction of the windfall. The remaining "saved
for a rainy day" cookie money had been Renee's start-
up fund.

The stairs creaked behind her. She turned. Flynn's
long, bare legs came into view as he descended. His
running shorts displayed his muscular calves and thighs
to mouthwatering perfection, and his sleeveless T-shirt
revealed powerful shoulders and arms. Desire flickered
to life inside her. She tried to snuff it out with little success.

His gaze raked her, making her self-conscious of her
old jeans, long-sleeved knit shirt and bare feet. "Good
morning, Renee."

"Good morning. Do you still run every day?"

"Rain or shine. Care to join me?"

Déjà vu. She smiled. "You know the answer to that
one."

He'd always asked. She'd always refused. She lik-
ened running to getting a paper cut—something she
avoided whenever possible. But the invitation was a
game they'd once played, and it worried her how easily
they had fallen back into the banter.

He tapped his hip. "I have my cell phone if you need
me. I left the number upstairs on the table." He nodded
toward the blueprint. "Did you make a decision?"

She took a deep breath and then a sip of coffee,
delaying the inevitable and maybe hoping for divine
intervention in the form of a better idea. "You're right.
Using the basement is the best option."

Satisfaction gleamed in his eyes. He nodded. "I'll
make the call to the contractor first thing in the morning.

I know one I trust implicitly. Monday afternoon we'll go out and look at tile, cabinets and countertops."

"Don't you have to work Monday?"

"I'll take the afternoon off. Come by the office after lunch and we'll leave from there."

That surprised her. He'd never taken time off from Madd Comm before, and he certainly hadn't liked her popping in and interrupting his day—a circumstance that had only reinforced his mother's snippy comments about him having other "more suitable" women.

"Look over the preliminary plans while I'm out and see if you want to make any changes."

"Your drawings are as wonderful as always." He'd had so much talent back then and shown so much promise that big firms had been trying to recruit him even before he had his certifications.

A frown flickered across his face. "I'll have to ask a licensed architect from my old firm to sign off on the plans."

"You do that." Maybe in talking to them he'd remember how much he used to love the work.

He crossed to the exterior door and opened it, letting in a cool rush of air. "I'll be back."

The door closed behind him, leaving her in silence—a reminder of the long, lonely days and nights she'd once spent in this house while Flynn worked. She couldn't help but believe their marriage would have survived if he'd stayed with his beloved architecture, instead of becoming the VP at the family firm. But because he'd minored in business administration and been groomed to work there until he'd rebelled and refused, he'd been familiar with how Madd Comm worked, and he'd been the only one considered for the job after their father's death.

She shook her head. The lo[...] enced back then wouldn't happen[...] allow it. She had her own business a[...] life and happiness would never ag[...] wrapped up in Flynn.

She took the last sip of her coffee, [...] blueprints and climbed the stairs. In the[...] have cooked breakfast while Flynn ha[...] she'd have had it waiting on the table whe[...] Cooking for him and doing things for him[...] with satisfaction. She debated raiding his re[...] see what ingredients she could find, but sh[...] This was not the old days.

Instead, she refilled her mug and sat down w[...] of paper. Starting up a new branch would be a[...] work, but she had experience under her belt now[...] needed to make a shopping list, a to-do list and a ge[...] list. Once she combined her lists and got an estim[...] from a contractor, she'd be able to tailor her budget.

The doorbell rang, breaking into her concentration. Had Flynn forgotten his key? Did he still keep a spare behind the ornate wrought-iron house numbers? She glanced at the clock. He'd only been gone forty minutes. He used to run for closer to an hour. But that had been years ago.

She rose and shuffled barefoot to the front door. The glass distorted the person on the other side, but not so much that she couldn't see her visitor was too petite to be Flynn. Who would visit so early?

Renee opened the door. Her mother-in-law stood on the doormat. Dislike crawled over Renee. Carol Maddox. There wasn't a polite way to describe her. "Hello, Carol."

was not jealousy. She had no right to be jealous if Flynn had found someone during their separation. To be jealous she'd have to still care. She didn't. "Does he?"

"Yes. You're wasting his time and yours. She's our kind. You are not."

"By 'your kind' you mean rich, rude and backstabbing?" The words popped out of Renee's mouth before she could curb them. While a part of her was horrified by her disrespect, another part took pride in the fact she'd finally stood up for herself with this bully. Civility had never worked with Carol. The harder Renee had tried to make her mother-in-law like her, the more obnoxious Carol had become.

Carol's eyes widened in surprise, then narrowed in calculation. "So you've finally grown a backbone. How commendable. But you're too late and it's not enough. You'll lose Flynn the same way you did before. He loves Denise and plans to marry her."

The cauldron of toxic feelings bubbled in Renee's stomach. Anger. That's all it was. Anger toward this hateful, malicious woman. "That might prove a little difficult since he's still married to me because *he* never filed the papers."

Carol stiffened. "An oversight, I'm sure. You may have him temporarily distracted, but whatever the reason you came looking for him, sooner or later he'll see through your innocent act to the opportunistic tramp you are."

Renee's nails bit into her palms as she fought to control her temper. She yearned to tell the supercilious witch that stud service and a desire to dilute the Maddox pedigree was the only thing on her agenda, but Renee bit her tongue. She'd promised to try to make the reconciliation look real.

During their marriage she'd been so afraid of losing

Flynn or turning him against her that she'd never told him about his mother's barrage of insults. Today she didn't have those concerns. In fact, if they were going to split up, it would be better if they did so before she invested her time and money in expanding CGC and before she became pregnant.

"FYI, Carol, Flynn came looking for me. In fact, my moving back in was completely his idea. He drew up these plans for me to convert the basement into my business." She gestured to the blueprints. "And he asked me to have his baby. We're discussing trying right away since we've already wasted seven years."

"You're lying."

"I'm not. We're going to make you a grandmother. Granny Carol. How do you like that?"

The horror in the older woman's eyes didn't alter her chemically paralyzed face, but Carol looked as if she had caught a whiff of something malodorous. "If you care anything for Flynn, you'll go back where you came from and let him find happiness with Denise. He loves her," Carol repeated, "and the marriage plans are already under way."

The arrow hit its target with another burning barb. *Don't let her get to you.*

She stared her mother-in-law down. "And if you care anything for your son, you'll keep your nasty comments to yourself. Because I'm warning you, Carol, if you dare to play any of your spiteful, undermining mind games with me this time around, I won't hesitate to tell your son how hateful you've always treated me."

"Tell me now," Flynn said from the basement doorway, startling Renee. Slapping a hand to her chest, she spun around.

"Flynn, I didn't hear you come in."

"I used the basement entrance. I thought you might still be down there studying the plans." He walked deeper into the room, his blue gaze unblinking on hers. He didn't even acknowledge his mother's presence. "Tell me what you meant about my mother playing spiteful undermining games."

Renee winced. "How long have you been standing there listening?"

"Long enough to know you kept something from me during our marriage. Something important. Spit it out, Renee. All of it."

She wasn't a tattletale. Her words had been mostly bravado, and one glance at Carol's superior, daring look told Renee her mother-in-law didn't believe she had the guts to reveal the truth. Resignation and determination settled over Renee. If she didn't follow through with her threat, then Carol would walk all over her. Again.

Speak now or forever hold your peace.

Flynn had never gotten along well with his mother, but still… She *was* his mother.

Renee tried for diplomacy. "Your mother has never made it a secret that she didn't approve of me or our marriage. If you recall, she tried to talk you out of marrying me. That's one of the reasons we went to Vegas."

"Was she rude to you when we were married before?"

Renee hesitated. But again, she couldn't back down without losing ground. "Yes. And more than once she implied that you weren't working late. That you were with another woman. This morning she informed me you were in love with someone named Denise and that I needed to step aside and let you marry her as planned."

"What?" The genuine astonishment on his face said more than any denial could have. Carol was lying.

"I take it you haven't proposed to Denise?" Renee asked, just to be sure.

"No. How could I propose to another woman when I'm still married to you?" He closed the distance between them and lifted a hand to firmly cup her face, then he looped an arm around her waist, pulled her close and kissed her so tenderly her knees nearly buckled. He pulled back until his forehead rested on hers. She smelled fresh sweat and Flynn's unique scent—a devastating combo. Her heart pounded.

What was he doing?

"You are the love of my life, Renee. I don't want any other woman." His soft voice and gentle touch melted her, but pure command filled his eyes. He leaned forward and nipped her earlobe.

"Play along," he whispered in a rush of warm breath across her skin.

She shivered as arousal raced through her like water through a broken dam. Did he mean what he'd said? He couldn't. Otherwise, why would he have stayed away until now?

When he kissed her again, she kissed him back. Not because he said to, but because she couldn't have resisted even if she'd wanted to.

Trouble. SOS.

Slowly, he released her, then turned to his mother. He loomed over Carol, his body language threatening. "Get the hell out of our house and don't come back. You are no longer welcome here, Mother. If I find out you've so much as looked hard at Renee, you'll regret it."

"You can't possibly believe her?"

"I have no reason not to. Renee has never lied to me. You, on the other hand, have a habit of doing and saying whatever it takes to get your way."

"Flynn, I do not lie," Carol protested.

He grasped his mother's bony arm and frog-marched her out of the room. "You just did when you said I was going to marry Denise." Flynn's voice carried from the foyer. "She and I dated twice, nothing more, and you know it. There won't be a wedding. I already have a wife."

The front door opened, then slammed a moment later. Flynn returned to the kitchen, his steps heavy with anger.

"Thank you, Flynn."

"Why didn't you tell me?"

She plucked at the seam of her jeans. "I didn't want you to have to choose between me and her."

He assessed her through narrowed eyes. "You thought I'd take Mother's side."

Yes. "She is your mother."

Heaven knows she'd been forced to cover for hers often enough.

"Because she's my mother I know how she operates. She's a bitter, unhappy person who infects those around her with the same ill temperament. I'm sorry she worked her sorcery on you, but if you'd told me, I would have put a stop to it."

Touched by his support, Renee pressed a hand over her heart. Would he have been as supportive if she'd told him about his mother's nastiness years ago? Moot point. She'd never given him the chance. "You had enough on your plate then, trying to learn a new business and grieving for your father."

"I insist on total honesty from you this time, Renee. I'll settle for nothing less."

"And for better or worse, you'll get it."

Flynn looked into the pleading blue-green eyes of Celia Taylor.

"Flynn, please let me put together a pitch for Reese Enterprises. Other Maddox ad execs may have failed, but I know I can get to Evan Reese."

"What makes you so sure?" The male ad execs of Madd Comm believed the attractive redhead used her looks to lure new clients. Flynn wasn't so sure. While Celia was beautiful, she seemed too sharp to rely on something so superficial. And while her looks might be a great asset, appearance alone couldn't deliver the goods the way Celia did time and time again.

"I've met Evan several times over the past few months. We've…connected."

He frowned, not liking the sound of that. "Is this going to be a conflict of interest?"

She shook her head and her hair swung over her shoulder. "We're not dating or sleeping together, if that's what you're asking."

"I wasn't, but thanks for clarifying. We can't risk pissing off a potential client due to a romance with one of our staff going sour."

"Not an issue. I'll put together an irresistible package—if you'll give me a shot."

Her enthusiasm and confidence were admirable and made him inclined to believe her. "Why come to me, instead of Brock?"

"Because Brock is so obsessed with landing Reese Enterprises that he only wants to send in someone like

Jason, our current Golden Boy. Brock's not willing to let an underdog like me take on the task."

Celia was right on one count. Brock was obsessed, and if his brother's grouchy attitude and the bags under his eyes were an indicator, Brock hadn't been getting enough sleep. Flynn had been meaning to talk to him and remind him how destructive tunnel vision could be. Brock's broken engagement and Flynn's failed marriage were perfect examples.

Speaking of his marriage, his wife was due any minute. He checked his watch and rose. "Give it your best shot, Celia. I'll speak to Brock on your behalf and let him know you have my support."

Celia sprang out of her chair, raced around the desk and threw her arms around Flynn's neck. "Thank you. You won't regret it."

"Make sure of it or Brock will have both of our heads."

The exterior of the seven-story building housing Maddox Communications on ritzy Powell Street hadn't changed, but Renee's feelings about entering the building had undergone a drastic transition. The joy and anticipation she'd once experienced when meeting Flynn at work had turned to trepidation. Entering those doors meant entering a web of deception.

Flynn hadn't been born when his father had purchased the soon-to-be demolished Beaux Arts–style building back in the seventies, but Flynn had told her the photo documentation of the renovations had fascinated him from an early age and launched his interest in architecture. He'd never intended to join the family advertising agency. He'd wanted to design buildings. And then his father had died and his priorities had changed.

She neared the doors and her muscles tensed. Trendy restaurants and retail stores still occupied the first floor. In the past Madd Comm had occupied the second through sixth floors, and the top floor had contained a penthouse suite with a huge roof garden. Who lived there now?

Renee entered the building and made her way to the elevators. A dark-haired muscular man about her age held the doors open for her. Renee stepped into the cubicle. "Six, please."

He nodded and pushed the button. "Are you a Maddox client?"

"No." She hesitated, unsure who this guy was or what Flynn had told his coworkers and clients about her. But Flynn had said to make the marriage look real. *Let the games begin.* "I'm Renee Maddox, Flynn's wife."

If her response surprised him, his gray eyes didn't show it. "Gavin Spencer. I'm an ad exec for Maddox. Flynn's a nice guy."

"Yes. He is." She shook the hand he extended. "It's nice to meet you, Gavin."

The elevator shot up, then the doors opened. Gavin motioned for her to precede him. "Nice meeting you, Renee."

She stepped out. A slim woman with short brown hair sat behind the reception desk directly ahead of Renee. Swallowing the nervous lump in her throat, Renee scanned the area while she waited for the receptionist to end her phone call.

In the waiting room white sofas faced two monstrously large flat-panel TVs streaming advertisements—Madd Comm's work, no doubt. The stark white walls and acrylic tables combined with the black oak floors gave the place a contemporary edge. The other walls held extremely colorful modern paintings, some new to Renee like the TVs, some not.

"May I help you?" the receptionist asked in a cheer-leader-chipper voice.

"I'm Renee Maddox. I'm here to see Flynn."

The woman's eyes widened. "I'm Shelby, Mrs. Maddox. Flynn told me to expect you. It's great to finally meet you."

"Thank you. You, too, Shelby. Should I head back or is Flynn with someone?"

"He doesn't have an appointment, but I'll call and let him know you've arrived."

Before she could dial, an attractive auburn-haired pregnant woman approached from the offices section. The receptionist perked up. "Lauren, this is Flynn's wife, Renee," she blurted as if she couldn't contain the news.

Smiling, the newcomer stopped. "Hello, Renee. I'm Lauren, Jason's wife."

Renee scanned her memory and came up empty. "Jason? I'm sorry, you'll have to forgive me. I haven't been here in…a long time. I've been living in L.A., so I'm a little out of the loop."

"I'm new here, too. I just moved from Manhattan last month. Jason is an advertising executive. We'll have to get together sometime and do lunch."

Lauren seemed warm and friendly and Renee could use a few friends in the area. She had no intention of repeating her past mistake of isolating herself. Also, an insider could give her an idea of what Flynn's life was like now. "I'd like that."

"Good. Can I reach you at Flynn's home number?"

"Yes. Or you can call my cell number. I'll be in and out a lot." She dug into her purse for a business card and passed it over. "I'm trying to open a branch of my catering business here in San Francisco, and I have a lot of running around to do while I set up."

"Something else we have in common. I'm opening a branch of my graphic-design business here, too. We will have a lot to talk about. But I have to run to an appointment now. I'll call, okay?"

"I'm looking forward to it."

Lauren ducked into the open elevator and the doors closed. The receptionist seemed to be hanging on their every word and then startled as if she'd suddenly remembered she was supposed to be calling Flynn. "I'll let Flynn know you've arrived."

"Don't bother. I'll just go back." Renee's heels tapped on the wood floors as she made her way to the east corner office as she'd done so many times before. This time her pulse raced with nervousness instead of excitement. If Flynn had changed offices, this would be embarrassing.

The chair behind his PA's desk was empty, but Cammie's nameplate on the desk told her at least Flynn's assistant hadn't changed. Cammie had been with him since his first day at Madd Comm and Renee had always liked her.

Flynn's door stood open. But Flynn wasn't alone. A woman with long red hair had her arms around his neck.

Shock stopped Renee in the outer office. She struggled to inhale, but her tight chest resisted.

You're not jealous.

Oh, yes, you are.

And that did not bode well for her mental health or the temporary nature of this assignment.

Four

Was Flynn involved with another woman?

The poison Flynn's mother had spread in the past and again yesterday percolated through Renee, filling her with doubts. About him. About herself. About their plan to make a baby.

Renee's throat tightened. Could she stand knowing that while he held her, made love to her and impregnated her, he was thinking of someone else?

The woman backed away from Flynn and bent to scoop a file folder from the visitor chair. "Thank you again, Flynn. I'll keep you abreast of the project."

"Do that. You'll need to run the proposal by Brock before pitching it." Flynn glanced up and caught sight of Renee. Her expression must have given away her chaotic thoughts. His gaze sharpened on her face.

Smiling tightly, Flynn came around his desk, took

Renee in his arms and kissed her without warning. She stiffened automatically as his hot body pressed hers and his warm, firm lips moved over her mouth. Conscious of their audience, she had to fight to relax and look as if this was a regular occurrence.

Getting used to being touched by him again was going to take some work. Not that she didn't enjoy his kisses and caresses. She did. Too much. Even now, despite the other woman in the office, desire curled in Renee's belly and her pulse fluttered wildly. But she had to hold herself in check. She couldn't let herself crave him or surrender to him the way she once had.

Flynn eased back and turned her toward the woman. "Celia, I'd like you to meet my wife, Renee. Renee, this is Celia Taylor, one of our ad execs."

The beautiful redhead grimaced. "Sorry about the hug, but he just let me break the good ol' boy barrier. I got a little excited."

Celia's words and contrite expression seemed genuine. And what Renee had seen after the hug had looked innocent enough. There had been no lingering body or eye contact. Tension leeched from her knotted muscles. "It's nice to meet you, Celia."

"Nice meeting you, too, Renee. Now, thanks to your husband, I have a lot of work to do, and trust me, that is not a complaint. Excuse me." She left, the quick tap of her heels receding down the hall.

Renee looked everywhere but at Flynn while she grappled with the strength of the emotions that had hit her when she'd spotted him in another woman's arms. No matter how much she might want to deny it, she had been jealous. That was not good.

The office looked exactly as it had seven years ago—

right down to the photograph of the two of them on the shelf and the remains of a half-eaten lunch on his desk. Back then she'd brought him meals time and time again because he often forgot to eat, and in a matter of a few months he'd dropped a lot of weight despite her TLC.

Flynn looked her up and down, making her heart skip. "You're right on time, and you look great."

"Thanks." She brushed a hand over her light, garnet-red, cowl-neck sweater and simple black twill trousers. "You have several new staff members. I met Gavin in the elevator, Shelby in the lobby and Lauren on the way in. I forgot who she said she was married to, but it was someone I don't know. She suggested we have lunch together soon."

"She's married to Jason Reagert, another ad exec. You'll meet him later. But Lauren is a good contact. She can probably recommend an obstetrician since she's pregnant."

Panic skipped down Renee's spine. She wanted a baby. She even wanted Flynn's baby. But tying herself to a man who made her weak still scared her more than a little—especially given her emotional reaction moments ago. Was she strong enough to endure a temporary marriage and a permanent link through a child without breaking and turning to alcohol again? "I'll keep that in mind."

"You'll have to join us next time the office staff goes out after work to meet everyone at once."

"What did you tell them about me…about us?"

"That we'd worked out our differences and our trial separation was over."

Her gaze flicked to the photo. "Have you had that sitting there the whole time?"

He frowned. "No. I dug it out of storage when you agreed to move back in."

For some reason that seemed like the perfect answer to soothe her rattled nerves. He hadn't been pining for her, but he hadn't thrown away the picture. She still had the box of mementos from her marriage that she hadn't been able to part with, either. As much as she'd wanted to put Flynn out of her mind, she hadn't been successful.

If you haven't succeeded in forgetting him in seven years, will you ever?

The nagging voice in the back of her head didn't ease her worry that this entire plot could blow up in her face.

Renee's head spun with combinations of paint samples and fabric swatches, cabinet configurations and countertop surfaces as she shoved her key into the front door Monday evening. Just like old times. And it felt good. Eerily good.

She'd forgotten what an effective team she and Flynn made, but today, watching his sharp mind work and his eyes gleam with intelligence and excitement as they discussed the basement conversion had brought all those bittersweet memories stampeding back.

"Do you want to eat in the kitchen or in the den in front of a movie?" he asked from behind her.

Another flashback. In fact, the past had hung over her like a rain cloud the entire day. Déjà vu moments had unexpectedly spattered down on her. Some like big, fat warm droplets and others like icy cold drizzle. There had been no escaping the deluge of memories.

In the early days of their marriage they had ended many a day of labor by having dinner on the sofa in front of the TV with an old movie. Sometimes they'd even watched the entire film before climbing all over each other. But most of the time they'd missed the last half because they were too absorbed in making love to hear it playing in the background.

Her skin flushed and her hands trembled as she dropped her keys into her purse. "Kitchen."

His gaze held hers and his pupils expanded, telling her he remembered, too. Her chest tightened. She couldn't get enough air into her lungs and had to open her mouth to breathe. "Flynn, don't."

He moved closer, then lifted his hand and cupped her face. "Don't what? Tell you that I want you? That I can't stop thinking about losing myself in the softness of your skin and the scent of your body, in the heat of you?"

A shiver of desire rippled over her.

"Don't tell you that I've barely slept for the past three nights because I've lain awake listening for sounds of you moving around our house?"

She'd done the same, listened for him.

"Your house," she corrected automatically.

"Our house. Your touch is in every room, Renee."

She told herself to back away, but her legs refused to move. "I'm not ready, Flynn, and I'm still not convinced this is a good idea."

"It's a good plan. A baby. *Our* baby. Us doing what we do best. Making a home. Making love."

The husky pitch of the last phrase only increased her desire. But her defenses were too weak to give in now. Before they did this, she had to find a way to make this about sex and procreation, instead of making love. Gathering every ounce of strength she possessed, she ducked out of reach and hurried into the kitchen. He followed.

They'd stopped by their favorite Chinese restaurant for

takeout on their way home. She took the bag from him, set it on the table and opened it. The aromas of hot and sour soup, Yu-Hsiang pork and Hunan chicken and shrimp filled the air. But her appetite had taken a vacation.

"For this to work you have to want it, too, Renee."

"I do. I mean, I will. But not yet." She had to change the subject because she was very, very close to giving in, and that could be the death of her—literally. "I'd like to keep your design, but I think the island should be movable, instead of fixed."

"*Re*movable, you mean."

Uncomfortable with the edge in his voice, she bit her lip. "You always talked about having a games room or a home theater downstairs. You still might one of these days. Making things portable, instead of built-in would make that transition easier."

"You're keeping one foot out the door."

"What do you mean?" she asked, but she knew. He'd seen her ambivalence, her fear.

"Nothing nailed down. No permanent fixtures other than the required plumbing. You refused to sign the builder's contract today. He might have believed your excuse of double-checking finances, but I don't. Either you're in or you're out. Which is it?"

Stalling, she retrieved plates from the cabinet and returned to set them on the table. "I'm in. I think."

"Once we conceive this child, you can't change your mind. I will be a part of my baby's life—a part of *your* life for at least eighteen years and very likely longer."

That's what scared her. That and the fact that she'd almost signed contracts today committing to investing a substantial sum of money in Flynn's basement. Doubts had hit her as soon as she'd lifted the pen. The contractor had been understanding and agreed to give her a few days to think over his estimate.

"I know how long we'd be tied together, Flynn. Let's eat before dinner gets cold." *Coward,* her conscience gibed.

"Let it." He came up behind her and wrapped his arms around her middle and she jumped.

"It wouldn't be the first time." His palms spread low over her abdomen, pulling her flush against him, then his lips grazed her neck in that spot that had always driven her crazy. "Let's make a baby tonight, Renee."

Hunger for her husband raced through her and temptation chiseled away her will to resist. Her breaths hiccupped in, then shuddered out. She desperately sought any reason to resist. "I don't know if it's the right time of the month."

His hands caressed upward, stopping short of her breasts, then back down again to her hips. "Forget about timing. Focus on how good we are together."

He skimmed up her torso again, and her nipples tightened in anticipation, but he stopped short of them to trace the elastic band on the bottom of her bra before descending again.

Up. Down. Up. Down. With each rise her breath caught. With each descent she exhaled...in disappointment, it shamed her to admit. Despite everything that had happened in the past, she wanted his touch. *Craved* his touch.

But she wasn't ready. She wasn't strong enough. Why was that, exactly? She couldn't concentrate on the reasons this shouldn't happen yet, with his hands on her body. Flynn had always known exactly how to arouse her. Physically, they'd always been in perfect tune.

Up. This time he cradled her breasts, instead of leaving her hanging. His thumbs brushed across the puckered tips and her womb tightened. Why was she even bothering to fight? She was going to give in eventually, anyway. Wasn't she?

Down. She caught his hands, halting their descent, and lifted them back to where she needed them. Flynn rewarded her by simultaneously rolling her nipples with his fingers and scraping his teeth lightly along the shell of her ear. A shudder racked her.

She pushed her hips back against him and encountered his erection, rigid and hot against her spine. Her resistance crumbled. She turned in his arms, her hip bumping deliberately over his arousal and making him inhale sharply.

His nostrils flared, and then he stabbed his fingers into her hair, framing her head and holding her steady. His mouth covered hers. Their tongues clashed in a kiss as wild and passionate and breathtaking as any they'd ever shared. Each successive kiss and caress grew more urgent, more desperate. His hands skimmed down to cover her bottom and yank her closer.

She dug her fingers into his waist and held on until her head spun from lack of oxygen and disorientation. The past and the present blurred in a wash of want and hormones. But if she couldn't distinguish between reality and old fantasies, then how would she survive this relationship? Flynn had been her greatest joy, but also her greatest weakness. She ripped her mouth from his and touched her fingers to her still-tingling lips.

Desire darkened Flynn's eyes and his cheekbones. His palms branded her upper arms. "Make love with me, Renee. Now. Tonight."

Her heart battered against her rib cage and her mouth went dry. If she had sex with him now, there would be no turning back, no time to gather her strength. She'd be surrendering without making one single attempt at self-preservation. "I can't. I'm sorry."

And then she did exactly what she'd done seven years ago when she'd woken up on the sofa with two empty wine bottles lying on the floor and no memory of opening the second. She ran.

Flynn couldn't wipe the smile off his face. He'd awoken hard, horny and miserable as a result of last night's nut-knotting kisses, but he wasn't complaining. He considered the prelude to his nearly sleepless night progress.

Renee was almost his. It was only a matter of time before the chemistry between them became explosive.

Balancing the tray on one hand, he knocked on her door with the other. She didn't answer, but that didn't surprise him. Renee had always been a sound sleeper. He turned the knob and pushed.

She lay on her side, with the covers bunched at her feet. She'd always preferred to sleep without getting tangled in bedding. One long, bare leg was hooked over a pillow she clutched to her chest. Her position stretched the fabric of her nightshirt tight across her bottom, making it easy to determine she wasn't wearing panties. During their early days, he'd been her pillow, and her leg would have been hitched over his hip and thigh. And she would have been naked. His groin pulsed at the memory.

The temptation to wake her the way he once had—by caressing her skin, running his palm up her leg and smoothing over her round butt—was almost irresistible.

"Renee. Wake up."

She startled awake and rolled over, shoving her curls out of her face. "What? What's wrong?"

"Nothing's wrong. I brought breakfast."

Squinting, she scrubbed the sleep from her eyes. Knowing her as well as he did had its rewards. He took advantage of her usual morning fog to hustle forward and plant himself on the bed beside her before she awoke enough to realize she was giving him one hell of a good view. If he anchored the sheets in the process, making it impossible for her to cover up, he considered it a fringe benefit. She had to get comfortable around him again and the only way to achieve that goal was through exposure.

"Sit up."

Blinking owlishly at the tray, she scooted up against the pillows. "You cooked for me? You've never brought me breakfast in bed before."

He didn't miss the suspicion in her morning-husky tone. "Our relationship before was a little one-sided. You always cooked for me. But times have changed. If we're both going to be working, we're going to have to share the chores. Especially after the baby comes."

She bit her lip, worrying the soft, pink flesh and making him ache to lean in and kiss her again. But moving too fast could cost him the battle, so instead, he settled the tray across her lap and enjoyed the sight of her nipples tenting her thin sleep shirt. The little nubs drew his gaze like a power outage does looters and hit his gut with a brick of desire that splinted through him like a broken store window. He blinked and tried to focus on his goal—getting her to let down her guard. He nudged the coffee mug in her direction.

"I've adjusted the blueprints based on the comments you made yesterday."

She picked up a piece of toast slathered in raspberry jelly. "What do you mean?"

"You wanted temporary. I found a compromise."

She chewed her toast, then sipped her coffee. "Explain."

He slid the sketch out from under the plate containing her scrambled eggs, Canadian bacon and fruit. "Instead of built-in standard cabinets, the island will have legs. It will look like furniture and can be moved against the wall like a sideboard or out to the patio when necessary. But that means you'll lose the prep sink in the island. I've moved it to the corner."

Renee took the page from him. Her hair fell across her face as she bent to study the sketch. He caught a strand and twined a curl around his finger. Her chin jerked up. He tucked the lock behind her ear, taking the time to run his finger down the side of her jaw and over her pulse point. The beat quickened beneath his fingertip.

"You always did look good in the morning."

She leaned out of reach and put a self-conscious hand to her tousled curls. "My hair's probably a mess."

He shrugged. "A little messy. But that's always more interesting than a woman with every hair in place."

Her cheeks flushed, then her eyes narrowed on his. "Did you sleep at all last night, Flynn?"

Busted. "You know I can't sleep when I have ideas I need to get onto paper."

Sympathy turned down the corners of her mouth, then her attention returned to his rendition of the kitchen. "It's beautiful, Flynn, but the contractor has already given us his estimate."

"This early on it's easy to amend the numbers."

"It's a good idea. Thank you for making the changes. I'll, um, think about them."

He nodded. "Finish your breakfast. I have a meeting with Brock this morning. I'll be leaving in twenty minutes."

"Is everything all right?" He shouldn't be surprised she'd picked up on his tension. Renee had always been perceptive. And he'd been a fool to neglect her.

"He's obsessing about a client. I need to talk him off the ledge."

"You're good at that."

If he'd been better at talking sense into people, he would have been able to talk her out of leaving. But then, she'd given him no clue of her plans. One day she'd been there and the next she'd been gone.

"I'm good at a lot of things." His gaze fell to her breasts.

Her breath hitched and her nipples puckered. "If you'll excuse me, I'll take my shower and then deal with the contractor. You take care of your brother."

He patted her thigh, savoring the warm silkiness of her skin and fighting the urge to slide his fingers north into the warmth between her legs. Her quadriceps tensed beneath his fingers, reminding him of his goal—getting her pregnant.

But this was the one time he'd welcome failure on the first few tries. Hell, he wouldn't mind if it took a year…or two. As long as he had Renee in his bed he'd be happy.

"So Renee is back," Brock said as soon as Flynn closed the door marked CEO. "Why?"

"What do you mean why? I told you."

"C'mon, Flynn. Level with me."

"You don't believe she missed me and what we had and wanted to try again?"

"No. You burst in here eight days ago asking questions about your divorce out of the blue. Four days later Renee moved back into your house. The question is, what started that domino fall of events?"

He didn't intend to tell Brock—or anyone—the whole truth. Telling the truth meant admitting failure. "We still care about each other and we're going to try again."

His brother's expression turned from disbelief to disgust. "You're sticking with that lame story?"

"Yes."

"For the record, the rest of the staff may buy it, but I don't." Brock rocked back in his chair. "This isn't about your inability to accept you're fallible like the rest of us, is it?"

Tension invaded Flynn's spine. "I don't know what you mean."

"You have no tolerance for weakness or failure. That goes double when it's your own. I credit Dad for that. He rode you pretty hard."

Flynn had been a failure in his father's eyes. He knew it and accepted it. Brock, on the other hand, could do no wrong. The old resentments percolated beneath his skin, but he ignored them and focused on what had brought him to Brock's office. "Sounds like we're talking about you, not me. You can't let this Reese Enterprises thing go. You're obsessed."

"You're mistaken. You always blamed yourself for the failure of your marriage," Brock added. "You couldn't accept that Renee might have gotten tired of playing house."

Flynn's surprise that Brock had read him so well vied with his anger at the unjust accusation, but he wasn't going to be so easily distracted. Worry for his brother had brought him to the lion's den. "If you must rehash the past, remember one thing. You've already lost a fiancée because of your obsession with work."

Brock folded his arms. "Good riddance, but we were talking about you."

"You might have been, but I wasn't, and I'm the one who scheduled this meeting." He parked his butt in the chair facing Brock. "Judging by the matching set of baggage beneath your eyes, you're not sleeping."

"What, are you a psychiatrist now?"

"You need to get your mind off work and get laid. Find someone to take the edge off. Isn't there a woman you can speed-dial for an unemotional quickie?"

He could use a little of his own medicine. The trouble was, now that Renee was back, he didn't want anyone else, and even if he did, he couldn't risk a scandal that might cost them business.

Living with Renee was like walking a tightrope stretched between heaven and hell. One wrong step and he could fall and land on the wrong side of the rope. She'd insisted on sticking with her get-reacquainted stipulation, which resulted in him having one hell of a time concentrating on work.

The only upside: the lack of sheet time forced him to focus on less carnal aspects of his beautiful wife—like her new strength and confidence. Not to mention her recently acquired curves. A very sexy combo.

Brock pitched his pen onto the desktop. "Sex isn't the answer."

"Maybe not, but it relaxes you enough to get the blood flowing back to your brain."

A knock preceded the door opening a crack. Elle Linton, Brock's executive assistant, poked her head through the gap. Her gaze flicked between Flynn and

Brock and then settled on her boss. "Your next appointment is on his way up."

Flynn turned back to Brock and caught a quick glimpse of something on his brother's face he hadn't seen before. But then Brock blinked and straightened, his mouth reforming into a tense line, before Flynn could decipher the expression. "Thank you, Elle. Give me five minutes."

"Yes, sir." The door closed.

His own lack of sleep had him imagining things. Was there something between his brother and Elle? No way. Brock would never condone an office affair. Maybe thoughts of another woman had brought that hungry expression to Brock's face just before his assistant had knocked. Did he have a speed date in mind already?

Flynn rose. "Think about what I said. Get a little R & R before you crack up. I don't want your job."

"I'm fine. You watch your step. I don't want to have to clean up again after hurricane Renee blows out of town."

"Not going to happen." Flynn intended to make damned sure of it. He might be fallible and he did make mistakes.

But he never made the same one twice.

Five

Renee's cell phone vibrated in her pocket, making her jump. She grimaced at Lauren. "Oops. Sorry. My phone buzzed me."

Lauren waved her hand. "No problem. Go ahead and see who it is. Like me, you're waiting to hear from contractors and can't afford to miss something important."

Renee checked the caller ID. *Flynn.* Her pulse took a *ba-ba-boom* misstep.

"It's my husband." She had to force herself to say the H-word. In her head Flynn had been her ex for so long it would take some time to get used to his new/old status.

"Take the call. Believe me, if Jason called I'd answer."

"Thanks." Renee punched the button. "Yes?"

"Join me for lunch," Flynn's deep voice said, and her heart clenched in regret.

"Too late. I'm just finishing brunch with Lauren. As soon as we pay our checks we're going shopping."

"We'll do it another time." Did he sound disappointed? "Don't forget to get the doctor recommendation. See you tonight, baby."

That "baby" shimmied down her spine like a featherlight caress. Renee disconnected and pocketed her phone. As much as she liked Lauren and believed they could be friends, Renee had no intention of asking for an obstetrician's name, because a very insistent part of her subconscious kept yelling, *Run before it's too late!*

She dabbed her mouth with her napkin. "How long have you and Jason been married?"

"Three weeks," Lauren replied with a smile that lit up her face.

Surprise hiked Renee's eyebrows. "You're newlyweds."

"That, of course, leads to the next question." Lauren pointed to her baby bump. "Jason and I worked together in New York and had a brief affair before he moved out here for the Maddox job. It wasn't supposed to be more than that. The pregnancy caught me by surprise, and I debated not telling him. I was prepared to have my baby on my own. But when Jason found out, he wanted more. Our explosive chemistry returned and we got married." She winked. "He is pretty irresistible when he puts his mind to it."

Love and pregnancy combined to give Lauren's face a beautiful glow that Renee had read about but never seen. An itty-bitty twinge of jealousy nipped at her heels. She would never have that glow with Flynn. She couldn't afford to let herself love as deeply as she once had ever again.

"What about you and Flynn? You do realize you're the hot topic in the Maddox break room at the moment, don't you?"

Renee grimaced. "I suspected that might be the case. Flynn and I met, fell in love and ran off to Vegas eight years ago."

"I sense a story there."

Renee shrugged and decided it wouldn't hurt to share a little background. "Carol Maddox will never be a big fan of mine. She claimed I wasn't worthy of her son and said she'd boycott our wedding. Flynn and I took that option away from her by eloping."

"How did your family feel about missing the wedding?"

Renee winced. "I hated not having my grandmother there, but she understood, and all she wanted was my happiness. Since I loved Flynn she supported my decision."

"It was just you and your grandmother, then?"

"And my mother. But Mom…well, she's sort of in her own world." Lauren's brows lifted in a silent question. "She's a chef. Brilliantly creative, temperamental, self-centered—all the clichés you've ever heard about top chefs fit. So it was mostly Granny and me. But Granny was wonderful, so please don't think I'm a pity case. Far from it."

"Good to know. Do you mind my asking what happened to you and Flynn?"

A fresh wave of pain hit hard and fast. Renee glanced away. If she was over him, then why did it still hurt to think about those miserable months?

"After Flynn's father died, Flynn and I hit a rough patch and took a break. We're trying to work out our differences now." She believed she could trust Lauren and was tempted to ask her advice, but instead, she tucked the cash for her lunch into the vinyl folder with the bill and tactfully changed the subject. "Are you ready to overheat your credit card in the local stores?"

"Absolutely. I appreciate your willingness to tag along and offer your opinion. Most women's eyes glaze over when I start babbling about nurseries—unless they're pregnant." Lauren's mouth opened in surprise, and excitement widened her green eyes. "You're not, are you?"

"Pregnant? No. But Flynn and I are discussing it. We'd once planned to have a large family, so I don't mind looking."

"You said you were waiting on calls from a contractor, too?" Renee ventured as they strolled side by side toward the shop someone had recommended to Lauren.

Lauren nodded. "We're building an office behind Jason's home in the Mission District. It's a historic property, and we have to have an architecturally equivalent design to meet all the codes and regulations. Our simple addition has become quite a complicated endeavor."

Renee nodded sympathetically. "I know what you mean. Flynn and I plan to convert the basement of his Pacific Heights Victorian into a kitchen for my catering business. I don't want to do anything to violate zoning laws or devalue the property."

"It's a challenge to make new fit into old, but working so close to home will be worth it, especially after the baby comes."

Exactly what Flynn had said.

They arrived at a baby boutique catering to upper-class mommies-to-be. Renee followed Lauren in.

Inside the boutique each vignette portrayed a perfectly decorated nursery. Before she'd left Flynn, Renee used to wander through the baby departments of local stores, yearning for a family and someone to love. But she'd done her looking and yearning alone.

Then the oddest thing happened at the fourth display. A sensation of coming home settled over her like a warm blanket. She ran her fingertips over the rails of an oak crib with chubby, tumbling teddy bears painted on the head and footboards and tried in vain not to fall in love with the piece.

If the baby plan came to fruition, she had to have this furniture.

"Gorgeous, isn't it?" a saleswoman said.

"Yes." Renee looked around for Lauren, but her new friend had moved several displays deeper into the store.

"Each spindle is hand-lathed, and of course, the bears are hand-painted. It's a one-of-a-kind piece from one of our most talented and sought-after craftsmen. When are you due?" the woman asked.

"Oh, I'm not pregnant. Yet."

A polite smile stretched the woman's lips. "Ah. Then may I suggest that if you're going to wait until you conceive to make your purchase, you might not want to set your heart on this crib. This gentleman's work always sells within a week of being put on the floor."

Indecision twisted inside Renee. If she walked away now, she'd probably never have this set. But if she bought it, she'd be making a commitment to an idea that still terrified her. "I...I'd better catch up with my shopping partner."

The saleswoman's interest cooled. "Of course."

With turmoil tossing inside her like a stormy sea, for the next five minutes Renee shadowed Lauren through the store. Questions tumbled through her brain, distracting her from the task at hand.

"Renee, are you okay?"

"Can I ask you something?" She waited for Lauren's nod. "Starting a family, moving and expanding your business simultaneously is a lot to take on, and yet you seem so serene. Doesn't this much change at once make you nervous?"

Lauren chuckled. "Of course it does. And if I appear calm, it's an illusion. I adore my husband, and I can't imagine not having this baby or sharing the pregnancy with Jason now. My only concern is that Jason loves his work so much that he might miss a few things if I don't make sure he puts us ahead of business."

The words struck a chord deep inside Renee. "I understand that concern all too well. After Flynn joined Maddox he became a workaholic. I almost never saw him."

"I'll bet that contributed to your need for a break." Renee hesitated, then nodded. "For what it's worth, I make Jason take time out most weekends for a sail on his boat. That allows us some quality one-on-one time and gives me an opportunity to polish my painting skills."

The wicked glint in Lauren's eyes caught Renee's attention. "Do I want to pursue that topic?"

Lauren flashed a mischief-filled grin. "Probably not." She tapped a hand-carved toy chest. "What do you think of this piece? It's not too feminine, is it?"

"No. It's lovely." Renee realized she and Lauren were approaching pregnancy with polar-opposite attitudes. Lauren's pregnancy had been unplanned and yet she'd happily embraced the coming baby and the upheaval in her life. Renee, on the other hand, was trying to plan and control every detail and was petrified of failing and falling in love with Flynn again. She wished she possessed a fraction of Lauren's courage.

Lauren smoothed her hand over a quilt. "I don't want you to think I'm making light of your fears. I'm not. It's all terrifying—moving across the country, getting married, having a baby—but I choose to focus on the positives, and I refuse to live in fear of what *might* go wrong. There are no guarantees in life. Sometimes you just have to take a chance and believe that you can make things right."

The words wrapped Renee in a familiar embrace. "My grandmother always said the same thing."

"There you go, then. Great minds think alike." Lauren punctuated the words with a wink.

Renee had never known anyone wiser or stronger than her grandmother. When Emma's husband had gone off to war, she'd taken over running the diner and continued doing so after her husband's death in battle. She'd not only succeeded, she'd excelled.

Emma had raised a daughter alone and then stepped in to help raise her granddaughter when her alcoholic daughter couldn't cope. Renee had never heard Granny complain about the unfairness of life or how hard it was to keep a roof over their heads and food on the table. Renee wanted to be as strong as Emma.

Renee's spine stiffened as realization dawned. Carol Maddox was right. Renee hadn't had a backbone before. She hadn't stood up for herself or fought for what she wanted. But she had the strength to do so now. She could do this.

She wanted a baby, a family. And she wanted to expand her business. Flynn was offering her the opportunity to achieve her dreams. All she had to do was guard her heart for the next twelve to eighteen months or so and then divorce Flynn.

Just like her granny, she could have her baby, her career and keep her sanity. She wouldn't have to keep the San Francisco catering biz in Flynn's basement once it started making enough profit to cover a lease elsewhere. All she'd have to do is move it to a new location.

With so much to gain, how could she afford to say no?

A combination of trepidation and excitement filled Renee with three parts can-do attitude and one part yellow-bellied coward as she pulled into Flynn's driveway.

"Please don't let this be a mistake," she whispered as she shoved open the van door and slung her purse over her shoulder.

Commit to a goal and go for it, Granny's voice echoed in her head.

But she didn't have a clue how to approach her husband for a procreation-only get-together. In the past when they'd made love she hadn't minded initiating the encounters, but this time there would be no love involved—just sex and if she was lucky, a baby. She'd checked her calendar and the timing seemed right.

She slipped her key into the lock and let herself in the front door. The aroma of grilling beef reached her, making her mouth water and her tummy grumble. She stopped in surprise. Flynn was home? And cooking? "Flynn?"

"In the kitchen."

She dropped her bag, took a deep breath for courage and made her way to the back of the house. Her legs trembled like a virgin's. Crazy.

Flynn stood by the range, turning steaks.

"You're home early and you're cooking again."

He turned. "I had this great wife who spoiled me with delicious food. When she left I couldn't stomach the old bachelor fare of sandwiches or frozen stuff, and a man can't live by takeout alone. I had to learn to cook."

He twisted the cap on a bottle of sparkling water and filled two champagne flutes waiting on the counter. He brought one to her.

"Are we celebrating something?" How could he know she'd conquered her reservations and made a decision?

"The builder called. He said you'd signed the contract."

Oh. That. "Yes."

He chinked his glass to hers. "Congratulations. You'll have your new branch open in no time. May it be as successful as the first."

Her heart pounded against her chest wall. She took a sip, swallowed and then blurted, "I bought nursery furniture today."

Flynn's chest expanded on a deep inhalation. "'Bout damn time," he muttered and set his glass aside, then he took hers, too, even though she'd only had one sip.

He grasped her waist, his hands burning her through her knit dress, and pulled her body flush against his. "Wanting to hold you, touch you and taste you has been driving me crazy."

Her nervousness dissolved like sugar in boiling water—right along with her knees. She and Flynn had been good together. She should have known he wouldn't let this be awkward. The sex would be easy and natural, the way it had always been. All she had to worry about was protecting her heart.

He bent and kissed her, a soft sweep of his mouth

over hers, a gentle nip of her bottom lip, and then he settled in. His lips pressed hers apart and his tongue tangled with hers—slick, hot, wet and full of hungry passion. He tasted good, like the Flynn she remembered. Her heart raced as she ran her hands over his thick biceps, broad shoulders and strong back.

His hands skimmed over her, hitting every erogenous zone. She'd missed this. Missed him.

A timer beeped, intruding into her euphoric haze. "What's that?"

"Dinner," he muttered against her neck, then grazed the tender skin with his teeth.

Renee leaned back and met his passion-darkened gaze. "Looks like dinner is going to get cold."

A sexy, hungry smile eased over his lips. "Good plan. Give me two seconds."

He spun from her, turned off the burners and the grill. When he turned back, the need tightening his face made her gulp. He crossed the room in long, deliberate strides, and her heart rate doubled.

Flynn fisted the hem of her shirt and pulled it over her head. She gasped at the suddenness of the move. He stared down at her breasts and cupped them with his hands, sending a current of need straight to her core.

"I never thought it possible for you to be more beautiful than you were before. I was wrong."

She cupped his face and stroked his beard-stubbled jaw. "Thank you."

He bent and nuzzled her cleavage. The softness of his lips contrasting with the coarse rasp of his five-o'clock shadow caused desire to fist in her abdomen. He dusted a string of butterfly-light caresses across each curve until she ached for more. She arched to give him better access and to press her pelvis against his. His thick erection burned into her.

Reaching behind her, he released her bra and peeled the lace away, then captured a tight nipple with his mouth. Wet heat surrounded her sensitive flesh. He tugged with his lips, his teeth, his fingertips, forcing a moan of pleasure from her.

Heat radiated from her core. She raked her fingers through his soft hair and held him close. He knew exactly how she liked to be touched. Not too rough. Not too gentle. No one had ever been able to play her body the way Flynn could.

His fingers stabbed into the waistband of her slacks, making her gasp, and then the fabric loosened. The zipper rasped open seconds before he pushed her pants and panties to the floor. His palm coasted over her hip, her belly and then into her curls. Pleasure sliced through her. "Flynn."

Eager to have his skin against hers, she kicked her shoes and clothing aside. And again he pulled back a few inches to study her. His expanding pupils and quick breaths gave approval as he reached for the buttons on his shirt. "Beautiful."

A moment's self-consciousness swept her. "I've gained weight."

He hushed her with a brief, hard kiss. "Baby, your new curves make me hot."

A smile bubbled to her lips. "I'm glad. Hurry," she pleaded and tried to help him disrobe, but her hands tangled with his, slowing him down. Impatient, she abandoned his shirt to tackle his belt and trousers.

Her fingers fumbled with leather and metal, then he was as naked as she and it was her turn to feast on his wide shoulders, deep pectorals and washboard abdomen. She traced the thin line of hair bisecting his lower belly and disappearing into the denser crop surrounding his erection. She wrapped her fingers around his hard, satiny flesh and stroked, loving his grunt of approval and the blaze of his skin against her palm.

He scooped her up, swung her around and sat her on the table. His fingers found the slick seam of her body and massaged her swollen flesh, making her womb clench with want. She wound her legs around his hips and tightened her grip on his steely flesh. "That feels wonderful."

"Slow down, baby."

"I don't want to go slow." She wanted fast and furious, a sensation overload to crowd out thoughts, doubts and fears that this could be a mistake. Sex with Flynn felt so good, so perfect and so right it scared her. They were so instantly in tune it could have been yesterday, instead of a lifetime ago, that they'd made love in this exact spot. In this kitchen. On this table. While some meal grew cold.

She hooked a hand behind his nape, yanked him close and kissed him, pulling him with her as she lay back on the cool wooden surface.

Flynn's body blanketed her with heat. His thighs pressed hers apart and his fingers found her exposed center, then he took a nipple into his mouth, laved, sucked and nipped it while he manipulated her until a knot of tension twisted so tightly in her tummy that she thought she'd snap. He must know how close she was to the edge. He'd always been able to read her body language.

He worked his way down her torso, over her ribs, across her waist to her hipbone, then he circled her navel, alternately teasing and arousing her with soft lips and hot tongue and bristly chin. Renee's muscles wound tighter with each inch he covered. Then he found her center, sucked her into his mouth and flicked his tongue over her. She gasped at the intensity of sensation arcing through her. Release hovered just out of reach.

"Flynn, I want you inside me," she whispered and tried to guide him.

He lifted his head from her curls. "Not yet."

His chin rasped her tender flesh, making her toes tingle. And then he pushed her over the edge. Orgasm crashed over her.

His gaze locked with hers as she tried to catch her breath, then he captured her hands and carried them over her head, rising above her and pinning her to the tabletop. He stroked his penis against her, his silky hard flesh gliding over her slick crevice as he sawed back and forth. Each smooth advance and slow retreat moved her closer and closer to a second release until she teetered on the brink. Her muscles tensed and her back arched in anticipation. He paused with his thick tip at her entrance.

"Don't you dare stop now," she ordered hoarsely. Squeezing her legs around him, she lifted her hips.

"And if I do?" She felt him smile against her temple.

"I'll make you pay."

His chest shuddered against hers on a rumble of laughter, then he plunged forward, thrusting deep into her body and pushing the air from her lungs. He drove in again and again, and she lost command of her body. Orgasm fractured her, emptied her lungs and seized control of her muscles, making them jerk and spasm involuntarily.

Flynn buried his face in her neck. "I…can't… hold…on."

"Don't even try." She pulled her hands free, raked her nails down his back and nipped his earlobe in the way she knew would break his restraint. His groan filled her ear as he bucked against her and emptied into her.

An urge to hold him close and cuddle descended on her. But there was no place for lovey-dovey this time around. As her skin cooled and her respiratory rate returned to something approaching normal, the gravity of the situation descended upon her. They could very well have made a baby tonight, and if they had there was no turning back.

Fear made her heart pound. She'd been sure she could do this earlier. But that was before they'd made love and she'd lost sight of her goal. Get pregnant. Get out. Instead, she wanted nothing more than to make love with Flynn again. And again. She couldn't afford to let him become an addiction she couldn't live without. An addiction that could ultimately destroy her.

She pushed against his shoulders. "Let me up."

Chest heaving, Flynn slowly levered himself off her. His eyelids were heavy, his face relaxed and his hair... well, she'd wrecked it. The strands stood in dark, irregular spikes.

"Going somewhere?" A smile lifted one corner of his mouth, and the tenderness in his eyes made her tummy swoop alarmingly.

She couldn't care about him. She had to remember this was a simple case of supply and demand. A business transaction. She wanted a baby. He'd promised to provide one. But the warmth and wetness of their joined bodies felt better than any business transaction she'd ever conducted and far more personal than insemination at a clinic would have been.

She squirmed to get out from under him and snatched her clothing from the floor. This wasn't more than sex, was it? Of course not. She'd have to be a total idiot to risk loving him again. She needed space and time to get her head together. "I'm going to shower before dinner."

"Sounds good." He pulled up and refastened his pants as if he planned to join her—the way he once would have. "Alone," she insisted and fled.

Six

He'd miscalculated, Flynn realized as he watched his naked wife exit the kitchen, her round behind jiggling and her bare feet slapping the hardwood floors as she hustled down the center hall and up the stairs.

Hit-and-run encounters were nothing new to him. He'd had several over the past four or five years while he'd believed himself to be single, but having one with Renee left a void in his chest.

He scooped up his shirt and stuffed his arms in the sleeves. His theory that reminding Renee of how good they used to be would lead to a happy reunion had missed its mark. Now what?

He grasped the back of his neck and scanned the kitchen. Dinner. After she had her shower she'd come back down and they'd discuss the situation over bacon-wrapped, medium-rare filet mignon, buttered asparagus and the *ciabatta* bread he'd picked up at the local bakery on the way home.

When he gathered new facts, he'd recalculate his strategy, because apparently it was going to take more than great sex and good food to make her forgive and forget six months of neglect.

He turned to the stove, flicked on the grill to finish the steaks and the burner to steam the asparagus. The old adage "two steps forward and one back" seemed to apply. Today she'd signed contracts and bought baby furniture, committing to spend time with him. And they'd had unprotected sex. That realization hit him with a fresh rush of adrenaline. Could their cells be on a collision course already?

So where had the reconciliation train derailed? At what point had he lost her? He could have sworn she'd been with him right up until he'd made like a geyser and blown. He knew the sex had been good. Fast, but good. He'd felt her contracting around him as she climaxed.

He tried to correlate the data and couldn't make sense of the way she blew hot and cold. Fear of pregnancy wasn't the issue, since the baby had been her idea. And she planned to divorce him. That meant she couldn't be concerned about him abandoning her again. Not that he intended to let that happen.

He didn't like her holding back even though he was doing the same. But he had to be careful. He wasn't sure he could handle loving her as deeply as he had before and then losing her again. If he hadn't been able to lose himself in Madd Comm, he might not have survived. But that was the catch-22. Renee claimed his obsession with Madd Comm had killed their marriage.

By the time he finished grilling the meat, he had a

rough idea of how to move forward. Identify the problem. Own the problem. Solve the problem.

He plated the food, but there was still no sign of Renee. Did she plan to hide in her room for the rest of the night? He wouldn't let that happen. He loaded the plates on a tray and carried the meal upstairs. The strategy had gained him ground this morning. Why not try it again? Renee had once told him that her family equated food with love, and this time around he'd decided to show his commitment to her by feeding her—the way she'd once done for him. It was a language he knew she'd understand.

He knocked on her door. No answer. She could still be in the shower. He turned the knob and pushed. His gaze ran over her neatly made empty bed and on to the bathroom's open door. Empty. The shift of a window sheer caught his eye. One French door to the balcony stood ajar. Renee leaned against the outside railing facing the sunset. She had a quilted throw wrapped around her shoulders against the cool evening air.

He crossed the room and toed open the door. She startled and turned. He ignored the lack of welcome on her face and set the tray on the small bistro table. "Dinner's ready."

She didn't move away from the rail. "Flynn, I'm ovulating. I thought I might be…so I checked."

He sucked in a deep breath. "How do you check?"

"I did a test strip after my shower."

"They make tests for that?"

"Yes, and since it might already be too late to change our minds I need to know you'll respect the boundaries I've laid out."

He'd respect them—right up until he mowed them

down. He wanted his wife back, and he didn't intend to settle for less than a normal marriage. "Renee, I would never force you to do something you didn't want to do, nor would I ever use a child as a weapon against you."

"I'm glad to hear that."

"If you're ovulating now, how long is our window of opportunity open?"

Her gaze bounced around the room then back to his. "About three days."

That meant he had three days to let the magic between them soften her up. But each month she failed to conceive meant one more he'd get to keep her around and additional time to convince her to throw away her idea of a temporary relationship.

He pointed to the chair and waited until she sat. "I owe you an apology."

Her expression turned wary. "For what?"

"During the last six months of our marriage I used our home like a hotel room, only dropping in when I needed to shower or crash before my head exploded. And I treated you no better than a hotel maid. I took what you did for me and our home for granted, and I even left cash like a tip on the table for you."

Her brow pleated. "Flynn—"

He held up a hand. "Let me finish. My only defense is that I was afraid of failing my mother, brother and the entire staff of Madd Comm. In the end I failed you, someone much more important to me than any of them. I take full responsibility for the failure of our marriage."

Her lips parted on a gasp and then she quickly ducked her head and focused on the fingers she'd knotted in her lap.

What had caused her shoulders to hunch? Why had she flinched?

She exhaled slowly. A moment later she lifted her gaze to his again, looking at him through worried eyes under long, dense lashes. "Apology accepted. But that doesn't change our current situation. We'll have this baby and then we'll go our separate ways. I'm not looking for forever, Flynn."

Not what he wanted to hear, but he would change her mind.

"We'll take it one day at a time." He studied her face, her eyes and the tense way she perched on the chair. Renee was hiding something. But what?

He wouldn't rest until he found out what.

Making love with Flynn had been neither clinical nor emotionless—the way Renee had hoped and expected it would be. The thoughtful, romantic meal of her favorites that he'd prepared only exacerbated the situation.

Dining with him resurrected too many memories: good ones of sharing similar evenings and bad ones of sitting on the sofa in sexy lingerie and waiting for him to come home or sitting outside on this balcony drinking alone. That was one of the reasons she'd chosen this room—to remind her of how weak she'd been.

Did that make her a masochist? Maybe. But Granny had always claimed the only way to overcome a weakness was to admit it and confront it—something Renee's mother had never done with her alcoholism.

Renee lay down her fork, her tummy full but agitated, and focused on Flynn, his thick dark hair, his deep blue eyes, his determined jaw and delicious mouth. He abhorred weakness of any kind. Would he hate her if he discovered her secret? Would he try to turn their child against her?

The urge to run quickened her pulse and dried her mouth. She wouldn't find the space she needed to distance herself from Flynn in this house, not with the past suffocating her.

"I'm going home to L.A. tonight. I need to check on Tamara and lease a new van for the San Francisco branch."

He frowned. "You said you were ovulating."

Therein lay the complication. Her break would, of necessity, be a brief one. And then tomorrow night she'd come back and make lo—*have sex* with Flynn again whether or not she had her head together. But right now she needed the strength that only mental and physical distance could deliver.

Beneath the table she picked at the seam of her pants with a fingernail. "Twenty-four hours shouldn't matter. I'll come back tomorrow as soon as I've done what needs doing in L.A."

His gaze fixed on hers like crosshairs on a target. "If you leave now it will be past midnight when you arrive."

"Traffic will be lighter at this time of night."

His lips thinned, then he inclined his head. "Let me help you acquire the van. I know a salesman at a local dealership that I trust who'll give you a good price."

He'd always tried to take care of her, to protect her from difficulties. She had to make him understand she needed to stand on her own feet. "Flynn, I can negotiate a car contract without a man to help me. I've done it before."

"If you could wait a few days, I could clear my calendar and go with you."

She couldn't let herself become dependent on him. He was only a temporary fixture in her life. "The builder will be here soon, and I won't be able to get away. He's working us in between projects. I have to go now. Tonight."

Resignation flattened his lips. "Call when you arrive and before you leave to come home to let me know you're on the road."

His concern yanked at something inside her, reminding her of a time they couldn't bear being apart for more than a few hours and they'd bent over backward to please each other. But those days were long gone and they weren't coming back. She wouldn't let them.

"How was week one in purgatory?" Tamara asked from the opposite side of the kitchen work counter early Wednesday morning.

Renee dropped the sugared violet she'd been carefully placing on a petit four. "It's only been five days and it's not purgatory."

"Living with my ex would be."

"Your ex is an idiot. Flynn's a nice guy. Are you sure you can handle this weekend's wedding alone? I could come back Friday night."

Tamara's dark eyes widened and her jaw went slack in disbelief. "Are you insane? And don't change the subject. You know you don't have to do this baby-making thing. If you want a kid that badly, I'll give you one of mine. They're already housebroken and they adore you."

"Ha-ha. Aren't you the comedienne? You love your girls, so don't give me that nonsense. I'm the one who had to dry your tears when your youngest started school, remember?"

Tamara sniffed. "What can I say? I was used to her coming to work with me. I lost the little slave who lived to fetch and carry for Mommy."

Renee chuckled and used the tweezers to gently anchor more violets in the icing. She'd taken a risk on hiring Tamara as a kitchen assistant four years ago. At the first interview Tamara had warned her that her daughter Angela suffered from epilepsy, and after a few terrifying seizures at day care Tamara didn't trust anyone else to watch out for her special child. Tamara had assured Renee that Angela would be as quiet as an angel, and the name had stuck.

Angel had been a fixture in the kitchen from Tamara's first day on the job. Renee had set up a gated corner, complete with toys and a small crib, which allowed Tamara to work and watch her daughter. During lunch more often than not all of them had eaten outside so Angel could run around Granny's backyard.

The interaction with Angel had only increased Renee's ache for a baby of her own, and Tamara hadn't been the only one missing the little girl since she'd started kindergarten last fall. The toys and gate were gone now, leaving the kitchen and Renee feeling empty and lonely.

"I want a family, Tamara."

"You do realize that having a baby doesn't guarantee you'll have someone who'll love you back, right?"

Renee smothered a wince as the arrow hit home. "I'm not a high schoolkid. Yes, I know."

"And being a single parent is hard."

"I know that, too, but because of your stellar example, I know I can do it. Besides, you let me practice on your children, so I'm ready." She scanned the work surface. "What's left to prepare after these?"

"You're changing the subject again. But it's the finger sandwiches, if you must know. I won't do those until tomorrow morning. What about the witch-in-law? Is she still a factor?"

Renee rolled her eyes. There were times she regretted sharing so much with her assistant. "Persistent, aren't you?"

Tamara batted her lashes in mock innocence. "It's one of my charms. Spill it."

"Carol has already been over to spread her poison, but Flynn overheard and he threw her out."

"Wow. Impressive. Too bad he didn't have the balls to do that seven years ago."

Renee winced. "I never told him that his mother treated me like trailer trash."

Tamara gaped. "You should have. Are you sure you can handle this sex-only relationship? You certainly are quick to jump to his defense."

"Again, with your fine example, I know how to handle it."

"Pffft. My sex-only lifestyle is because there's not a guy out there I'd trust to raise my girls or one who doesn't bail when he finds out about them. But there is some freedom in knowing that you can enjoy a man without the hassles that usually come attached to one."

"I intend to do exactly that."

"Still…you should think very hard before deciding to raise a child on your own. It's a 24/7/365 job."

"I know." Renee didn't dare tell her assistant that the decision might already have been made, because she didn't want to answer the multitude of questions that would follow. "You're managing to raise two on your own."

"I have your help."

Renee shrugged. "And I'll have yours."

"What about the San Francisco branch? What will

happen to it once you have what you want? You're not going to stay in his basement indefinitely, are you?"

"Once the business is going strong I'll find a new location and then hire a manager. If all goes according to plan and I get pregnant quickly, then I estimate my baby and I will be back in L.A. permanently in less than two years."

Tamara paused with the pastry bag in her hand. "You can count on me. And don't forget to tell that husband of yours that if he hurts you again, he'll feel my rolling pin upside the head."

"Your rolling pin is safe. Flynn won't get the chance to break my heart again."

Flynn caught himself watching the clock Wednesday morning and counting the minutes until he could get out of this meeting. Work had once monopolized his thoughts, but since Renee had come back into his life, she'd taken over the top slot.

Only half listening to the discussion around the conference room table, he caught himself sketching her face in the margin of the report in front of him and shifted in his seat.

What time would she get home?

Would she even come back?

She'd appeared to have second thoughts about their bargain after the sex. Hell, she'd left town last night to avoid a repeat encounter. He would have loved to get her into his bed and make love to her again more slowly, taking the time to linger over each inch of satiny skin. He would have reacquainted himself with all his favorite places: the sensitive spot behind her knee where she often dabbed perfume; the dimples at the base of her spine that she hated; the ticklish arch of her foot.

But she hadn't been interested in round two. If she really wanted to get pregnant, wouldn't she have hung around to jump him again last night and this morning? It bothered him that she'd sent him a text message to let him know she'd arrived safely rather than call as he'd asked. Like some romantic, newlywed sap, he'd wanted to hear her voice.

He checked his watch again. He'd have a surprise for Renee when—if—she came back. She liked to do her exercising indoors. He'd ordered a treadmill and video setup for her so she could walk her miles and watch cooking shows simultaneously. The equipment would be delivered late this afternoon.

Brock continued explaining how the economic crisis had put the squeeze on potential clients' advertising dollars. Nothing Flynn as VP didn't already know. Then his brother switched to Athos Koteas's latest account-stealing stunts. Again, it wasn't a news bulletin that the Greek immigrant was a ruthless bastard. Madd Comm struggled to compete with Koteas's European connections and devious tactics. Good thing none of the old guy's three sons was as competitive.

"That's bull and you know it," Asher Williams, Madd Comm's CFO, barked in reply to something Brock said, making Flynn snap to attention.

What had he missed? Flynn scanned the tense faces around the table and tried to figure out what had set off the normally unflappable Ash.

"Ash, we have to make it work," Brock said.

"You're asking the impossible." Ash shot to his feet and slammed out of the conference room. Silence descended, broken only by Brock's muffled curse and the shuffling of papers and clearing throats of the ad executives around the table.

Damn. Flynn rose. "I'll talk to him."

He followed Ash out and down the hall to the CFO's office and knocked on the open door. "You okay?"

Ash's brows flatlined over his hazel eyes. "Brock's trying to squeeze blood out of a rock. It can't be done."

"I hear you. But we have to stay competitive."

Ash stared silently out the window, his back tense.

Flynn closed the office door. "Is this even about work?" The silence stretched. "Do you have something you need to run by me, Ash?"

"Melody's gone."

Another man with woman troubles. What was that old cliché? *Women, can't live with them, can't live without them.* They were a blessing and curse. "Temporarily or permanently?"

"I don't know."

"Any idea where she went?"

"Negative."

"Been there, done that, man. You have my sympathy. Will you look for her?"

Ash pivoted abruptly. "Hell no. We were never going to be anything but short-term, anyway. I've been paying her way through law school, but she's probably found another sucker."

"That sucks, man. Losing a woman you love—"

"I never said I loved her. I don't. I'm just pissed off."

"Right." Denial was a wonderful thing. Flynn had fed on denial and anger for years after Renee left. "If you need anything—even if it's a designated driver while you drink yourself into oblivion—I'm your man."

Ash's drawn and pale face stared back at him. The guy might claim he wasn't hurting, but his eyes told a different story.

Flynn imagined he'd probably looked the same when Renee left the first time. But that was then. He intended to right the wrong he'd committed and repair his marriage. And while he'd love to have a long-term relationship with Renee and have several more children with her, he couldn't afford to love as wholeheartedly as he once had.

He'd save his love for his child or children if he could talk her into more. At least they wouldn't leave him until college time.

Seven

Turning into Flynn's driveway in her new van shouldn't have been an aphrodisiac, but for Renee, it was. She knew they'd have sex tonight. And only sex. There would be no bonding. Just sweaty, satisfying, exhilarating fulfillment.

Familiar signs of arousal took control of her body: accelerated pulse rate, flushed skin, shortness of breath, excessive moisture in her mouth. Her hands shook as she pocketed her car keys and climbed the brick steps to the front door.

She let herself in and silence greeted her. She should have checked the garage for Flynn's car. And then she noticed the spicy, garlicky, tomatoey scent in the air. Something Italian. Mama G's lasagna? She sniffed again and smelled the yeasty scent of dough. No. Papa G's pizza. Renee's mouth watered for an entirely different reason, and her stomach rumbled in anticipation.

No one made pizza as well as Papa G, and she and Flynn had ordered many of them for takeout when their renovations had left them too grungy for dining out or too tired to cook.

"Flynn?" She followed her nose to the kitchen and found it empty. A note on the table caught her eye. Trying not to think about what they'd done on that table twenty-four hours ago, she snatched up the page and turned her back on the scene of the crime—the crime being in the heat of the moment she'd temporarily lost sight of her goal. A baby and a clean break.

"Come to the basement," Flynn had written.

Had he started work on her kitchen already? Dumping her purse on the counter, she hurried downstairs. He wasn't in the area designated for CGC. "Flynn?"

"In here," he called from the storage room across the hall.

She heard an old home-restoration program playing on the TV as she approached. At her touch, the door dragged over carpeting that hadn't been here seven years ago. She scanned the gym equipment filling the space. Some kind of weight equipment with four stations occupied the center of the room flanked by an exercise bike on a rubber mat on the left and an electric treadmill on the right.

Flynn stood in front of a wide, flat-panel television mounted on the wall. He wore faded jeans and a snug white T-shirt and work boots. A leather tool belt hung on his hips, accentuating his muscular butt. Her heart stalled at the sexy, familiar sight.

He turned and extended his arms. "What do you think?"

That he looked delicious.

He tossed a small black object at her. She snapped

out of her daze, caught it and identified a remote control. "I didn't know you'd turned this room into a home gym."

"I hadn't until today. You can watch your cooking shows while you work out."

Surprised and touched by his thoughtfulness, she gasped. "You did this for me?"

He nodded. "I ordered the equipment the day after you moved in. They delivered it today."

A little of the wall she'd built around her heart crumbled. This was the old Flynn, the one who'd routinely surprised her with thoughtful, considerate gestures or gifts. The one she'd fallen in love with so long ago. She swallowed to ease the lump in her throat and reminded herself to guard her heart.

"This is incredibly nice, Flynn, but I could have rejoined the gym."

"Your favorite gym closed. The closest facility isn't as nice, and you always hated fighting for a parking space."

She grimaced at the memory of how she used to seize on any opportunity to avoid exercise. But that had been back when she was young enough to eat anything and not gain an ounce. When she'd passed thirty her body had changed. As much as she liked the wisdom that came with getting older, there were some parts of maturing she could do without.

"Well, yes, but…you didn't have to go to this expense. Thank you."

He pointed to an empty corner. "There's room over there for a playpen or crib. For after the baby."

Her head spun with images of Flynn's hands splayed over her swollen belly, working out beside her while she tried to get back in shape, of him cradling their tiny infant in his big, gentle hands.

A knot of emotion rose in her throat. "I—I hope you'll use some of the equipment, too."

"I will. Especially this." He straddled the weight bench. His thick biceps flexed as he pulled down on the bar hanging over his head.

She wanted him. Like this. Relaxed. Sexy. The old Flynn.

Her feet felt weighted as she crossed the room to his side and bent to kiss him. He let her take the lead, let her move her lips over his, waited for her tongue to slip into his mouth and caress his before he responded without releasing the weight bar. His tongue dueled with hers.

Her pulse raced as she sucked his bottom lip into her mouth and gently nipped the tender flesh. He grunted his approval. She lifted her head. Passion widened his pupils, the black almost obliterating his blue irises.

He shook his head. "As much as I would love to take you right here, right now, we're not rushing tonight. This time I want you in my bed. Naked, wet and breathless."

Desire made her dizzy. "You have two out of three already."

His nostrils flared, then a dangerous, naughty smile curved his lips. "Dinner first."

He exploded off the bench and brushed past her, leaving her staring at his gorgeous backside. And hungry. But not for Papa G's delicious pizza.

She wanted Flynn as badly as she ever had.

Flynn's muscles were so tense he could barely swallow. Dinner had been one long foreplay session.

With an imp of mischief lurking in her face, Renee had lingered over her food, licking dots of sauce from the corner of her mouth and fingertips and nibbling on errant, gooey strings of cheese or fallen slices of pepperoni.

He wanted that mouth on him, that talented pink tongue licking *his* lips, instead of hers. The moment she pushed her plate away, he shot to his feet, grabbed the dishes and dumped them in the sink. The scrape of her chair brought him around.

She stood by the kitchen door. Sexual hunger darkened her eyes to almost purple. Without a word she peeled her sweater over her head, dropped it on the floor and then pivoted and sauntered down the center hall to the stairs—the same way she'd retreated last night, only this time her invitation was clear in every sexy sway of her hips.

He smiled at the familiar game, and the needle of his body compass pointed north. In the early days, coming home to a bra on the foyer floor had been one hell of a welcome and the promise of a hot night ahead. When they'd wanted to make love he and Renee used to leave trails of clothing like bread crumbs leading to their location of choice. But somewhere along the way, they'd quit playing with each other and merely coexisted in the same space.

The blame for that rested solely on his shoulders. He'd been the one too exhausted to accept her sexy invitations. The disappointment he'd seen on her face when he refused had led him to sleep at the office a bit too often. He'd been so afraid of failing at work he couldn't tolerate the possibility of failing at home, too. In the end, his fear had become a self-fulfilling prophecy.

But not anymore. He had control of all aspects of his life—all aspects except his relationship with Renee. And if he felt a mild sense of discontent, then as soon as he had his marriage under control, that dissatisfaction would disappear.

He sat down long enough to untie and remove his work boots and socks, and then he followed her. Her bra draped the newel post, a pink lacy scrap of almost nothing. He scooped it up and sniffed her scent. The fabric still carried the warmth of her body. He could see his fingers through the cups. Halfway up the staircase she'd left one shoe. A few treads higher he spotted the other. He shucked his shirt and draped it over the banister. It slid down. He didn't care. Her pants puddled on the landing. He dropped his on top of them, then paused.

Which bedroom? His or hers?

The pink panties hanging on his doorknob provided the answer. Grinning, he strode toward the trail marker and hooked the lacy garment with his finger. They smelled of her. He pushed open the door. Renee reclined on a pile of pillows in the middle of his big bed with one knee bent to hide her blond curls, but that didn't make the sight of his wife, curvy and naked on his sheets, any less inviting or arousing.

He dangled her lingerie from his fingers. "Next time I want to see you in these. Then *I'll* take them off you."

She licked her lips, and he could practically feel her tongue on his erection. Heat pumped through him. Her gaze raked him, pausing at his tented boxers. "One of us is overdressed."

He dropped her undergarments, shoved his boxers down his legs and kicked them aside, then slowly stalked toward the bed. Looking his fill, he stretched out on the mattress beside her, but he didn't touch her. Not yet. Once he did he wouldn't be able to stop. A flush of arousal pinkened her cheeks, chest and breasts. Her nipples contracted under his scrutiny, and her stomach quivered slightly with each shallow breath she took.

He ached to be inside her, to pound his way to release, but he'd promised himself he'd take it slow and remind Renee how amazingly perfect they were together before letting go.

He twisted a blond ringlet around his finger, then released it to stroke her cheek, her nose, the softness of her parted lips. "I've missed this. Us."

Her breath hitched. She captured his hand, guiding it to her breast. The soft globe filled his palm, the pebbled tip pressing into him. He rolled the point between his fingers, drawing a whimper from her. Her lids fluttered closed. Propped on one elbow, he bent and replaced his fingers with his mouth, leaving his hand free to explore her other breast, her smooth stomach, her long legs and damp curls. She was already moist and hot. Need fisted in his abdomen.

She arched into his fingers, but he didn't want to rush this, so he moved on, caressing the crease behind her knee, the curve of her waist, the sensitive spot beneath her arm and the dip of her navel. She shuddered, encouraging him to follow the same path with his lips.

Her fingers tangled in his hair, alternately gripping and releasing. Her toes curled against the sheets. He relished her scent, her taste, the softness of her skin against his lips and tongue.

She slid the arch of her foot up his calf and down again. Her free hand kneaded his back, then his butt before sliding toward his swollen flesh. Determined to keep her from rushing him, he kept his groin out of reach. She detached from his hair to trace the shape of his ear and to tease the hammering pulse point below with the light scrape of her short nails. Desire rippled over him. Renee had never been a passive lover. She gave as much as she received.

He grazed his teeth along her instep and her legs tensed. He circled her ankle with his tongue, then worked his way up the back of her leg to nibble on the bottom curves of her buttocks. Her muscles tightened. She twisted beneath him, winding her legs around him and rubbing her hot center against his thigh.

Palming her knees, he pressed her legs apart, leaving her open and exposed to his gaze, to his mouth. He licked her slick seam, making her jerk and gasp, and then he nuzzled her neatly groomed curls.

Her scent filled him with the anticipation of driving her over the edge, of hearing her cries and feeling her contract around him. Slowly. He found her center again with his tongue, flicking the hot pink nub, teasing her to the brink and then backing off. Paying close attention to the tension of her muscles, he repeated the process, smiling against her thigh at her frustrated groan when he left her hanging a second time. He urged her toward orgasm again, but before he could withdraw a third time, her fingers fisted in his hair.

"Please, Flynn."

Her breathless plea sent his blood south. His penis pulsed against his thigh, reminding him who was boss and urging him to get on with it. He slid his fingers inside her and she groaned. She was so wet, so hot and tight and ready for him that it took all his restraint to delay his own gratification.

He sucked her into his mouth, making her moan and arch, and then he stroked her with his tongue and his hand until her muscles squeezed his fingers and her cries filled his ears. Her climax shuddered through her. He barely gave her a moment to catch her breath between spasms before making her come again and again.

She sank into the bed limp as he tongued her navel, giving her a break before his next planned assault. Her hand gently caressed his cheek. She lifted his chin until their eyes met. "I want you inside me for the next one. Please, Flynn. It feels so good when you're inside."

Hunger charged through him. He couldn't resist any longer. He climbed over her, hooked her legs over his forearms and drove deep. Slick heat welcomed him, and then she clutched him with her internal muscles, and it was his turn to groan as his head nearly exploded with pleasure.

He drew back and sank in again and again. Her breasts, jiggling with each slam of his hips against hers, riveted him, and then he had to feel that movement with his hands. He cupped and kneaded her, tweaking her nipples while he rocked his hips.

Renee locked her ankles behind his back and clamped her hands on his shoulders, pulling him down for a kiss that nearly boiled his brain. She devoured his mouth in a clash of tongues and teeth. To stave off his own release, he tried to focus on her, on the stiffening of her muscles, on her dampening skin and on her panting breaths, but a fuse lit in his gut, and he ignited like a roman candle. He tore his mouth away from hers as a groan roared from him. Blast after blast of ecstasy rocketed through his extremities until he was nothing but spent ash.

His elbows buckled. He collapsed on top of her, cushioned by her soft breasts, then eased to her side and braced himself on an elbow so he wouldn't crush her. A fog of satisfaction invaded his skull and weighted his eyelids.

Hitching her leg over his hip so he wouldn't have to disengage from the slick sleeve of her body, he wrapped her in his arms. Nothing had ever felt more right.

This is what they should have been doing for the past seven years. Solo sex and impersonal relationships didn't come close to delivering this level of satisfaction. He and Renee belonged together.

And as his body cooled and clarity slowly returned, he made an interesting realization. His deal with Renee wasn't just about correcting a mistake. It was about winning—winning his wife back.

There was no way in hell he was going to let her walk out of his life again. The passion was too intense. He would use whatever means necessary to keep her here. It was time to turn up the heat.

Excitement bubbled through Renee's veins Thursday evening as she stood on the patio outside the basement watching the workers pack up their tools for the day.

Everything was coming together much faster than the months of chaos she'd endured during the renovation of her grandmother's house. When Flynn flexed his influential muscles, work got done at an amazing rate. Yesterday he'd set up her gym, and today the permits had been issued and the work on her new kitchen had begun.

"How did the first day of construction go?" Flynn asked from behind her, startling her. Her heart *baboomed* wildly as his arms encircled her waist and his lips brushed her jaw. She hadn't expected him until later…if at all. Shadows of the past crept over her.

She turned quickly, simultaneously stepping out of his embrace. He looked powerful, charismatic and successful in his immaculate charcoal-gray suit, but she preferred him in the khakis and dress shirts with the rolled-up sleeves that he wore when he worked for the architectural firm, or the faded jeans and T-shirts he donned for renovation.

Memories of last night's passionate encounter rushed forward, but she muscled them back. Sexual satisfaction did not guarantee happiness, which was why she'd sneaked out of Flynn's bed as soon as he'd fallen asleep, and then she'd awoken early this morning, raced to her new gym, climbed on the treadmill and donned a pair of earphones so she could be working out when he came downstairs before work.

Yes, she admitted, she was taking the coward's way out, rather than discussing a situation that scared her.

Focus on the project, a much safer topic. "The basement tile has been laid. Tomorrow they'll grout, and then Monday the cabinets will be delivered and installed."

He strolled to the door to look around. "Looks good."

She caught herself checking out his broad shoulders, straight spine and tight butt, and forced her attention elsewhere. But diverting her gaze didn't derail her quickening pulse or the warmth pooling behind her navel. "I'm going to paint this weekend."

He faced her again, but she avoided his eyes, fearing he'd see her hunger she couldn't control. "You didn't contract the crew to do that for you?"

"No. Doing it myself saves money and gives me time to think." Time to plan and try to figure out exactly how their peculiar agreement would work out. She should have plotted the whole deal on paper—preferably in her lawyer's office with legal backup, but Flynn's need for secrecy had prevented that. "Besides, I like painting."

A smile tilted one corner of his mouth. "I know. I'll help you paint."

Butterflies took flight in her belly. Coming on the heels of the phenomenal sex, working side by side with Flynn would be a trip down memory lane she didn't need. "I can do it."

"I know you can, Renee. I doubt there's anything you can't handle when you set your mind to it, but I have a stake in how this project turns out."

The reminder that this was his house sobered her—exactly what she needed—and reminded her to ask her attorney to make sure everything she and Flynn had agreed upon was spelled out in their divorce agreement when the time came. "Yes, of course you do."

"I meant I want CGC to be up and running before your pregnancy makes it difficult for you to deal with the setup."

His thoughtfulness melted a tiny chip of her heart. "I may not be pregnant yet."

"But you will be. Soon."

The sensual promise in his words made her heart and womb contract. "I don't know what kind of strings you pulled, but the contractor thinks I'll be ready to fire up the stove by the end of next week."

"Then I'm glad I brought home a client list for you."

She blinked in surprise. "What?"

"I mentioned CGC to a few people and they're interested in talking to you about catering jobs. One wants an appointment ASAP for an emergency fill-in job."

He worked fast. "I wish I'd had you around when I started CGC. It wasn't nearly as easy to pick up clients. I pounded on a lot of doors and had a lot of rejections.

"Once the construction is completed I'll still have inspections to get through, but I need to work up an advertising plan and hire a few part-time employees."

"I can recommend a reputable employment agency to screen your applicants, and you have connections at Madd Comm for your promotional plan."

His generosity made it more difficult to keep her emotional distance. "Thank you. But Maddox isn't in my budget."

"We'll see about that." He lifted a hand and tangled his fingers in her hair. Renee's muscles locked, trapping the air in her lungs and making retreat impossible. "You have something in your hair."

He plucked at the strands, but he didn't release her after he'd tossed whatever it was aside. Instead, he cupped her head and held her as he bent to capture her mouth. Alarms shrilled inside her as his lips sipped from hers, stirring a response she wanted to deny but couldn't.

Flynn plied her mouth with gentle tugs, then when she gasped, his tongue swept inside to tangle with hers. His palms skated down her arms to rest in the small of her back, then he pulled her forward until her body rested against his. His heat suffused her.

She couldn't let herself love him again, but she couldn't stop the wanting. Kissing him felt so good, so familiar, so right. But it wasn't. Giving in to the passion he evoked was a dangerous act, like walking a tight wire without a net.

Push him away, a voice warned, but her neurons ignored the command. Her hands splayed on his chest. She felt the steady thump of his heart beneath her palm. Why hadn't she ever found anyone who could arouse her the way Flynn did? With nothing more than a kiss he made her pulse race and her knees weak.

A truck door slammed nearby—probably one of the workers. Flynn eased back, reluctance clear on his face, and checked his watch. "I'm supposed to take you to the Rosa Lounge for cocktails with the Madd Comm staff."

To continue the farce. The more people he introduced her to, the more he'd have to explain her absence to when they went their separate ways. "What is the Rosa Lounge?"

"A bar on Stockton. The team meets there for celebrations."

"Flynn, I'm not sure including me in your celebrations with your coworkers is a good idea. When I leave—"

"That's a long way off. I'll deal with it if it happens. If we want this reconciliation to look real, then you'll join me."

"*When* it happens. I hate lying to everyone."

"Would you prefer I call Brock and have him tell the staff we've decided to turn in early?"

Her cheeks heated at the implication and so did that coal in the center of her pelvis that Flynn seemed to be able to ignite at will. Would they have sex again tonight? Did she want to? *Yes.* The strength of her desire for him scared her.

He stroked her cheek, tucking a strand of hair behind her ear. "Lauren will be there."

Renee winced as he unintentionally twisted the knife of guilt inside her. Yet another person being deceived. She liked Lauren. They had a lot in common, both being transplants and opening new branches of existing businesses, and she hoped they'd be sounding boards for each other.

But what choice did she have except to play along?

She gestured to her jeans and casual sweater. "I'll need to shower and change."

And then she'd face Flynn's fellow Maddox employees and pull off the best acting job of her life. For her future child's sake, everyone had to believe the fairy tale Flynn had chosen to tell.

Eight

Renee cataloged the dimly lit bar as she entered with Flynn on her heels. Small, trendy, high-end clientele, and judging by the specials written on the blackboard in fluorescent green marker, expensive.

Flynn's hand snaked around her waist, and his lips and warm breath touched her ear. "Head for the tables in the back."

To onlookers his embrace would look intimate, but in reality he'd issued a command in a low, don't-argue-with-me tone, and his firm grip ensured she wouldn't chicken out and run.

She made her way down the center aisle between the large bar taking up most of one wall and the Rosa Lounge's green, glass-topped tables with tall, black-lacquer bar chairs lining the opposite. The voices reached her even before she spotted the long table where a half-dozen well-dressed twenty- and thirty-something patrons sat.

Lauren's auburn head lifted. She spotted Renee and Flynn and waved. Conscious of other heads turning, Renee fought off her nervousness and returned the gesture. One familiar face stood out in the crowd. Brock's.

Renee's stomach muscles seized. Brock, like his mother and father, had never been crazy about Renee, which made Brock's holding on to the divorce papers a bit unusual. He should have been eager to get rid of her. She wasn't sure she believed the tale he'd told Flynn about feeling guilty about breaking up the marriage. Brock rose from his seat at the head of the table and approached her.

"Renee. Welcome back." His eyes and voice were as cool as his handshake. Had Flynn told Brock the truth? Had he told anyone?

"Thank you. It's…good to be back," she added, since it was probably expected of her.

Flynn's arms encircled her waist, and he spooned her back from shoulders to knees with the muscled planes of his body. A wave of awareness and warmth washed over her as he leaned forward until his slightly bristly cheek pressed hers. "Everybody, this is Renee. My wife."

A chorus of hellos rained on her, then Flynn added, "You remember Celia and Lauren."

"Yes. Hello again." Both women's welcoming smiles seemed genuine.

"To Brock's right is Elle, his executive assistant. To Lauren's left is Jason, one of Madd Comm's ad execs and Lauren's husband." Renee nodded at each new person, since Flynn didn't release her to shake hands. "Next is Ash, another ad exec, and you've already met Gavin."

The names came so fast she hoped she could remember them. "Hi, everyone. Thanks for including me tonight."

She slid into the empty chair Flynn pulled out for her. Flynn shifted his chair close enough for his leg to press hers beneath the table. He offered her a menu with one hand and stretched his other arm along the back of her chair, then he twined a lock of her hair around his finger and gave a gentle tug.

She shivered. Renee's nape had always been ultra-sensitive—a fact Flynn knew all too well. She glanced up to see Celia, Elle and Lauren watching. Lauren winked and snuggled closer to Jason. Elle's gaze flicked to Brock and lingered before turning back to her menu. Was she reading Brock's expression to see how the boss felt about Renee's return?

The waitress arrived. "What can I get you?"

"A Diet Coke, please," Renee said.

"Bushmills," Flynn replied, naming the Irish whiskey he'd preferred for as long as she'd known him.

Celia leaned forward. "No martini? The Rosa Lounge is known for them."

"You're not pregnant, too, are you?" Elle asked.

Alarm trickled through Renee as all eyes focused on her. "Not that I know of."

She added a smile and hoped everyone would let the topic pass.

"Renee and I always wanted a large family. Maybe this time around we'll make it happen."

Flynn's words sent her heart crashing against her rib cage and brought her shocked gaze to his. A tender smile eased over his lips as he stroked her cheek with his knuckle. If she didn't know this was an act, she'd swear the love softening his eyes was real.

He'd wanted to make the reconciliation look believable, and he'd taken a giant step in that direction by laying their plan on the table for everyone to witness their success or failure.

And they would fail, she reminded herself. She would walk away—no matter how convincing Flynn might be in the role of the doting lover. Her sanity depended on escaping as soon as she'd fulfilled her end of their bargain.

Escaping before she broke.

A steady drumming beneath Renee's ear nagged her awake. She fought her way out of the sleepy fog and grappled for her bearings.

Friday. Tile grout.

But she didn't want to move from her snug spot. Warmth anchored her to the mattress. She opened her heavy eyelids and a male chest filled her vision. Her pulse jumped on a rush of adrenaline as she identified Flynn's bed, Flynn's arms around her and Flynn's erection pressing the thigh she'd hooked over his hips.

She shouldn't be here, but she must have fallen asleep after sex last night. Great sex. Exhausting I-can't-come-anymore sex. The kind they used to share back in the days when they couldn't get enough of each other.

Last night at the Rosa Lounge Flynn had used the ruse of their reignited love to touch her at every opportunity. He'd played with her hair, stroked her arm or shoulders and sneaked caresses on her thighs beneath the table, knowing that as per their agreement, she couldn't object. Even though she'd been aware he was shamelessly taking advantage of her predicament, he'd still had her so turned on by the time they reached the house last night that they'd barely made it inside the front door before ripping off each other's clothing.

She'd promised herself she'd leave his bed as soon as her legs regained the strength to carry her down the hall to her room, her shower and her bed. And yet here she was, with her limbs entangled in her husband's and his scent clinging to her skin.

And she didn't want to leave. That was exactly why she must. But she didn't want to wake Flynn. Didn't want to face him. Not after the way he'd played the besotted, possessive lover so convincingly in front of his brother and coworkers that she'd almost believed he still loved her.

Good thing she knew his love had died a very long time ago. He'd proved that time and time again by choosing not to come home.

Trying to slow her quick breaths, she slowly separated herself from him. She was almost free when his arms tightened, yanking her back and erasing the narrow gap she'd created between them. Her heart lurched.

"Going somewhere?" he asked in a gruff, sexy voice that rumbled through her like a passing train.

"I need to get dressed before the construction crew arrives."

He inhaled deeply and stretched, pressing his torso more firmly against hers. His hand swept down her back and curved over her bottom, stirring up a hunger that should have been more than satiated.

"Flynn, let me up."

He lifted slightly to look at the alarm clock, then sank back onto one elbow. "We have thirty minutes."

The husky intent in his voice made desire coalesce in her midsection. "I'm probably not…fertile anymore."

His palm skimmed upward over her hip, her waist, to cup her breast and thumb the nipple. A skewer of need pierced deeply and her flesh puckered. He nuzzled her temple. "You don't need to be fertile for me to make you feel good."

A pulse pounded deep inside her, and a craving for the satisfaction he could deliver swelled in her tummy. She fought it and shoved against his chest. She couldn't allow herself to become desperate for his attention ever again.

"Flynn, we're not supposed to be doing this unless the timing to conceive is right."

"There are no written rules for our agreement."

"Maybe there should be."

He held her captive with his passionate gaze and powerful arms for several more seconds as if debating changing her mind. Part of her wanted him to. And that part was the very one she had to ignore.

He relaxed his hold. "Run if you must."

She stiffened. "I'm not running. The builders will be here soon."

She scrambled from the bed and searched the floor, the bed, the room for something to cover her nakedness, but he'd removed her clothing downstairs. Short of dragging the sheet off his long, lean body or raiding his closet, she was out of luck.

She crossed her arms over her breasts and backed toward the hall. "I'm going to take a shower."

He sat up in bed. The sheets bunched around his naked hips, leaving his muscular chest and washboard abs on display—a mesmerizing view. "Tonight we'll move your stuff in here."

Panic knocked her breath from her lungs. "Flynn, I'm not sharing this room with you."

"When is the nursery furniture going to be delivered?"

She dampened her suddenly dry lips. In the excitement over her new workspace, she'd forgotten her purchase. "M-Monday."

"We'll paint the guest room this weekend before tackling your kitchen and have it ready by the time the furniture arrives." He tossed back the covers and rose in a rippling exhibition of firm, fit and aroused male.

Her fingers curled against the need to test his length and thickness. She blinked, tore her gaze from his morning erection, but she couldn't as easily banish the memory of how he'd felt in her hand, her mouth and her body mere hours ago. "What part of 'I am not sharing with you' did you not understand?"

"I heard you, but moving you in here is our only option."

"The third floor—"

"Isn't ready. The floors still need to be sanded and refinished." His gaze prowled from her head to her breasts, hips, toes and then returned at an even more leisurely pace.

Her skin prickled in response. She wanted to cover up. She wanted *him* to cover up. Concentrating when they were both naked was beyond her capabilities. "The builder—"

"Won't have time. I asked. He has to finish your kitchen by next Friday and return to his previously scheduled jobs."

She cradled her lower belly. "There's no rush. We don't know if there *is* a baby yet."

"There's no need to drag our feet. If we convert the front room into the nursery, we can work on the third floor together and get it right—the way we did with the rest of the house."

His words called to the primitive, nest-building part of her. "I'll have time to work upstairs until the bookings start coming in."

"You'll have bookings beginning next weekend."

Once more his words sent her reeling. "I won't have the permits."

"The first job is a small one. No permit required. You can work from my kitchen or the client's. Call Gretchen today and find out what she needs."

"Who's Gretchen?"

He strode into the bathroom, calling over his shoulder, "A friend."

Something in his tone made the hairs on her nape rise. She followed him and caught his gaze in the mirror. "A *girl*friend?"

His expression blanked and his hands flexed around his toothbrush. "She's a woman with connections who can give you the exposure you need to get your name out there."

His avoidance of an answer told her what she needed to know. A swarm of something ugly and uncomfortable buzzed inside her. She wasn't jealous. She was just… unsettled at the realization that once she left, there would be other women in Flynn's life. In her baby's life. Somehow that just hadn't been considered when she'd agreed to this deal.

The mirror reflected their nude bodies back at her, making her feel even more exposed. "Does she know we're still married?"

"That's irrelevant."

"Is it?" Was this Gretchen person his lover?

"Renee, don't make a big deal out of nothing."

She had no right to protest. And why was she standing here arguing when she needed to get ready? "I'm going to shower."

He captured her hand, his palm warm against hers. "You can shower here. With me."

Her breath hitched. If she stayed, any showering would be done *after* they made love again. His erection made that clear. Shared showers—with her arms braced against the tile, her legs splayed and Flynn taking her from behind, with his wet, soapy hands caressing her breasts—used to be one of her favorite ways to start the day. But not today.

She yanked free. "Flynn, don't make this into something it's not."

"And that is?"

"A real reconciliation. I am not sharing your bedroom or your bathroom."

"That's what you say, but this—" he flicked a fingertip over an erect nipple "—this says you want to."

An arrow of desire hit the bull's-eye. Turning on her heel, she retreated to the only sanctuary she had in this house—the guest room—and closed the door behind her. She sagged against the panel.

She'd been jealous twice now.

Being possessive was not the way to keep her distance. For all intents and purposes Flynn was merely her sperm donor by orthodox means. Nothing more.

And she wanted it that way.

The other woman could have him.

"But not until after I'm finished with him," she groused as she marched toward her bathroom.

The idea of him climbing from another woman's bed and into hers repulsed her. But that had absolutely nothing to do with her heart. Her only concern was her health, she assured herself. She didn't want Flynn giving her or her baby something contagious.

Renee couldn't sleep. She stared at the shadows dancing on her bedroom ceiling Friday night and willed the tension to ease from her overwrought body, but her mind kept racing with thoughts of the baby, her business, Flynn.

Especially Flynn. And the way he made her feel. How could he still get to her after all this time and all the heartache she'd endured at his hands?

She rolled over and fluffed her pillow. The clock inched toward midnight, then past it. This was how the trouble had started last time. Her drinking had begun with a simple nighttime glass of wine to help her unwind while waiting for Flynn to come home. Then it had progressed to a second glass to help her get to sleep.

She wasn't going to fall into the same trap this time. If she couldn't sleep she would find something constructive to do. But what? Play with recipes? No. Banging around the kitchen might wake Flynn. Exercise? No. That would work her up, rather than wind her down. She could paint the basement. She'd bought everything she needed this afternoon.

Decision made, she rolled out of bed, pulled on a pair of old jeans shorts and a T-shirt. She didn't bother with a bra. No one would see. Then she pulled her hair into a scrunchie and eased open her door. Only the sounds of the old house settling broke the silence. Good. Keeping an eye on the open door to Flynn's darkened bedroom, she crept down the stairs without turning on any lights, avoiding the third tread that squeaked. Being familiar with the house had its advantages.

When she reached the basement she sighed in relief at arriving undetected, then hustled to the supplies in the corner. She opened and stirred the paint while debating her options.

Tonight she needed monotonous, easy work. She'd save cutting in along the wood trim for tomorrow when her mind and her hands were steadier. After pouring the thick liquid into the tray, she coated the roller and then reached for the nearest wall. The sticky smacking sound of the paint rolling over drywall filled her with satisfaction, and the repetitive motion soothed her and allowed her mind to wander.

Marking her territory had always been important to her. Throughout her childhood and her early teens she and her mother had moved often, as her mom followed the jobs and earned her reputation as a temperamental but gifted chef. When Renee had turned thirteen, Lorraine had decided having a teenage daughter around made her look old and sent Renee to live with Emma. Renee had been thrilled at the prospect of putting down roots, but at the same time apprehensive about changing schools again.

Granny had made a party of it by inviting over the neighbors' teenagers to help paint Renee's bedroom, providing Renee with instant friends and a place to call home. That's why painting Flynn's Victorian had been so significant. Painting her space made her feel like she belonged and might not leave.

Wrong.

Bad memory. Tension returned to her muscles. She stepped back to study the ten-foot square she'd covered with French Vanilla paint.

"Good color," Flynn said behind her.

She jumped, almost dropping the roller, and turned. Flynn wore his boxer shorts and nothing else. "What are you doing up?"

He strolled closer, stepping from the shadowy area at the base of the stairs and into the brightly lit room that would become Renee's kitchen. The basement was cool, and his nipples tightened into tiny points. "I could ask you the same."

She shrugged. "I couldn't sleep. I decided to put my surplus energy to work."

"Good idea." He crossed to the pile of supplies.

"What are you doing?"

"Getting a brush."

No, no, no. "Flynn, it's one o'clock in the morning. Go back to bed."

"I will if you will."

If she quit now and retreated to her room, she'd only go back to tossing and turning and worrying.

"Could you at least put on some clothes?" How would she concentrate with all that taut golden skin, those washboard abs and ropy muscles on display?

"Not tonight. I'll have to search for clothing I don't mind getting paint on."

"But—"

"I've painted in less, Renee. So have you."

Memories hit her like a runaway trolley car. More than once she and Flynn had draped a sheet over the windows and painted in the nude. They'd had some of their happiest and most passionate moments speckled with paint.

"I'll cut in," he said as he filled a small bucket with the creamy hue.

She couldn't stop him from helping, but she didn't

have to watch him. She turned her back on him, refilled her roller and resumed her task. Struggling to maintain her focus, she covered another square yard, and then Flynn parked the stepladder beside her and climbed, putting his bare, hair-dusted muscular thighs and firm derriere directly in her line of vision.

She closed her eyes and took a fortifying breath. It was going to be a long night, and sleep…well, it wasn't going to make an appearance anytime soon.

Flynn flexed and stretched in her peripheral vision as he painted along the ceiling. She angled her body away from him, but the smooth ripple of his muscled shoulders and arms pulled her gaze back again and again. Arousal smoldered in her middle. How had they ever managed to get any work done before?

For almost an hour they painted side by side with only the hiss of the brush and the roller breaking the silence. It felt good, like the old days, when simply being in the same room had been enough to keep a smile on her face.

"What made you decide to have a baby now?" Flynn asked after they'd relocated the drop cloth and other paraphernalia to the second wall.

She stalled by refilling the paint tray and then her roller. "CGC is successful. I have time to focus on other things."

"But the real reason is…?"

She should have known she couldn't fool him. "What makes you think there's more to my decision than that?"

"Is something wrong physically to make your clock start ticking with such urgency that you were willing to pick a stranger out of a catalog to father your baby? We both know how unsettled you were not knowing anything about your father."

The concern in his voice touched her. "I'm in perfect health. I wouldn't have a child if I didn't plan to be around to care for it. But I'm tired of coming home to an empty house. With Granny gone…" Loss squeezed her throat, choking off her words. She waited until she had control of her emotions before continuing. "I always wanted a family. Waiting for Mr. Right isn't working, and I refuse to settle for Mr. Right Now."

Wasn't that exactly what she'd agreed to with Flynn? The only difference was she knew he'd be a good father. "And my assistant's daughter started school. Tamara used to bring Angel to work every day. I loved playing with her, and I miss her."

"I missed you after you left."

Surprise snatched her breath. She lowered the roller. "I'm surprised you even noticed I was gone."

His blue eyes locked on hers. "I noticed."

"You didn't come after me. You didn't even call." She winced. She hadn't meant to let that slip.

"Your note said, and I quote, 'Please don't contact me.' I had my pride. And frankly, I was angry."

"Why?"

"Because I expected you to stick it out, 'for better or for worse,' and help me through the rough patch."

Guilt burned in her belly. She wanted to take him in her arms and assure him he hadn't been the problem. But she couldn't. "You left me first, Flynn. Even though we still shared the same address, you abandoned the job you adored and me."

"I didn't have a choice. You did."

Yes, she'd had options. She could have stayed and lost herself. And then she'd have lost him, too. She'd decided it would be better to make a swift, clean break and quit him and the liquor cold turkey. "I had to go."

"Why?"

She shoved her roller across the wall, keeping her gaze fixed on the lines of paint. "Does it really matter? The past is over."

"What are you hiding, Renee?" he said an inch from her ear.

Her muscles snapped tight. If Flynn learned the truth and she wasn't already pregnant, he might refuse to give her the baby she desperately wanted. Her mother was an alcoholic. Renee could have easily become one. Their baby might carry that tendency in its genes. She was flawed and she didn't want Flynn to see her as damaged goods.

She stepped away from the heat of his bare torso under the guise of adding paint to her roller. "You're imagining things. I think I'll work another hour and finish this wall. If you're tired of painting you can head for bed."

"I'm in for the long haul. I always was."

She looked at him and held her tongue. He wouldn't have stuck around if he'd discovered the truth about her. Her mother's long line of lovers had proved time and time again that not even love could conquer the killing effects of alcoholism.

Nine

Over the next two hours Flynn focused on the cadence of Renee's roller strokes, biding his time as he plotted his next move.

As her agitation faded, the sticky sounds of paint application slowed from rapid sweeps to slow and unsteady stabs. In the past ten minutes he could tell her will to get the job done was the only thing moving her exhausted arm.

He lowered his brush and studied the droop of her shoulders. "Let's call it a night."

She startled and turned. "The room needs a second coat."

He put down his brush, crossed the room and pried the roller from her hand. "Let's have breakfast, catch a few hours of sleep and then apply the second coat."

A worry line pleated her brow. "But—"

"Renee, it's 4:00 a.m. We're both starting to lose precision." Like him, she'd always been a perfectionist. She'd understood his spending hours over the details of a blueprint because she could lose herself the same way in a recipe.

She studied the closest wall and a small dime-size spot she'd missed. "I guess so."

He brushed a lock of hair from her tired, violet eyes. "We have the entire weekend ahead of us. Your kitchen will be ready by the time the cabinets arrive on Monday. I promise."

So would the nursery, if he had his way, and Renee would be sleeping in his bed. Permanently. It might take a little finesse, but he would win this time.

"A hot shower would be nice." She rolled her shoulders as if they were stiff, and his fingers flexed in anticipation. But while he'd love to fill a hot bath for her and join her there for a slippery massage, she wasn't ready for that step.

"Go for it. I'll clean up here and get breakfast started."

She panned the painting supplies through eyes only half-open. "Are you sure?"

"I'm sure. Go."

He watched her climb the stairs, admiring her rounded bottom and smooth, pale legs. Renee didn't tan. She never had. She claimed her tone went straight from cream to lobster-red with no in-between. But he didn't care. He'd always loved her ivory skin. Tracing the lines of her breasts, inner arms and belly with his tongue had been one of his favorite pastimes. His groin pulsed at the memory.

Tamping down his unsatisfied need, he quickly put away the painting supplies, then climbed the stairs and washed up. He extracted the food he needed from the fridge and pantry and set to work on what had once been Renee's favorite breakfast. Was it still?

Fate had a twisted sense of humor. He and Renee had traded places. In the past he'd been the one who couldn't quit until a project was finished. Renee had been the one to supply him with food and urge him to rest. Giving up had never been a part of his nature. His fault-finding father had made sure Flynn always aimed for perfection. When he'd fallen short his father had relished pointing out every flaw.

Twenty minutes later the house smelled like cinnamon, melting butter and maple syrup, and Flynn had breakfast waiting on the coffee table when Renee entered the den wearing sweatpants and a T-shirt. She'd put on a bra this time, unfortunately. He'd enjoyed her beaded nipples in the cool basement almost as much as he'd enjoyed the peeks he'd caught her taking at him.

Knowing she was still attracted to him worked in his favor. He planned to agitate the chemistry between them until he achieved the desired reaction.

Her damp curly hair dragged across her shoulders, giving her a sleepy, freshly scrubbed look that called to his tired brain cells like reveille. She inhaled. "Do I smell apple-cinnamon pancakes?"

"You left your recipe card in the drawer."

"I haven't had them in years. Not since—" She bit her lip.

"We made them together?"

"Yes." Their gazes met and the shared memory stretched between them. His "help" in the kitchen had usually been more of a distraction and a hindrance. He'd pass her the ingredients she requested until his hands wandered into more intimate territory and the meals were temporarily put on hold for hot sex.

Her cheeks flushed, and she abruptly averted her face. "And is that coffee?"

"Decaf. We need sleep. You can have the real stuff after our nap."

She lifted a mug from the table and sipped, her eyes closing. "I almost fell asleep in the shower."

"It wouldn't be the first time." A smile tugged his lips. Until Renee he'd never met a woman who could work so hard she'd fall asleep as soon as she stopped moving. He'd caught her dozing in the shower numerous times.

He handed her a plate. "Eat."

"Thanks." She took a bite of pancake. "Mmm. Exactly the right amount of cinnamon."

When they'd cooked the recipe together in the past, the brown sugar and maple syrup had often ended up being licked off bare skin. Their kitchen had seen almost as much action as their bedroom.

Her lids grew heavier as her plate emptied. By the time she finished she was almost asleep sitting up. He took her dish from her and set it back on the coffee table beside his. She started to rise. He caught her hand. "Sit tight while I clear this away."

"Flynn, you don't have to wait on me."

"Consider it my turn."

Her lips parted as if she wanted to argue, but then she nodded and sank deeper into the cushions, almost limp with fatigue. He rose, gathered the breakfast dishes and carried them to the kitchen. He took his time loading them in the dishwasher and then returned to the den. As he'd expected she'd fallen asleep sitting up. He smiled at the success of his strategy, then debated his next move. As soundly as Renee slept, he could carry her upstairs and tuck her in without waking her. But waking in his bed would put her on the defensive.

He sat beside her and eased her over. She sighed, tucked her hands beneath her cheek and settled her head in his lap. Just like the good ol' days. Now all he had to do was convince her to move down the hall to his room and the battle would be all but won.

Someone had put hot rocks on her eyelids, Renee decided as she struggled to cut her way through the fog clouding her brain. And she needed a new pillow. This one was hard. And hot. And the down tickled her nose.

Down? You're allergic to down. Move before your face swells like a red balloon.

She forced her lids open and blinked against the bright sunlight streaming through the windows, trying to clear her vision. Her "pillow" resembled a man's thigh. Flynn's thigh.

Like rocks gaining momentum in an avalanche, her heart bounded into a faster rhythm as the chain of events leading up to her ending up with her face in Flynn's lap replayed on her mental movie screen.

The hands on the antique clock across the room pointed to noon. She must have fallen asleep after eating. This wasn't the first time she and Flynn had napped together on this sofa. But that was then. Now she had to be more careful. She knew how disastrous falling into a false sense of security with him could be, which was why she hadn't wanted to completely relax her guard and sleep in his bed.

Holding her breath and trying not to wake him, she

eased upright and stood. His bare chest continued rising and falling evenly. Flynn looked peaceful and relaxed tipped into the corner of the sofa with his dark lashes fanning his cheeks and the lines of stress smoothed away. A lock of hair fell across his forehead. The urge to comb her fingers through the lush strands and brush them back almost overcame her caution.

She turned away from the temptation. A piece of paper on the end table beside his lamp had caught her eye. Her slowly waking brain identified a drawing on the back of an envelope. She lifted it and her breath caught.

Flynn had sketched out a baby's nursery complete with a crib and mobile dangling above it, the dresser and even the toy box. She'd shown him the photo she'd taken of the furniture with her cell phone, and he'd accurately depicted the details in excruciating detail.

There was no mistaking which room of the house he'd placed the furniture in. Her room. The French doors leading to the balcony gave it away.

Flynn had always been a talented artist, but he'd usually limited his drawings to architectural designs. Though most of his work had been done on a computer, he'd liked to pick up a pencil when working out the rough idea.

She stroked a finger over the curving runner of a rocking horse, and emotion clogged her throat. Looking at this, she could almost believe he wanted a baby as much as she did. A baby who might have his ink-dark hair and bright blue eyes. A precious little boy or girl that would give her the family they'd once planned to share.

A hollow ache swelled in her chest. She wanted Flynn's baby probably more now than she had the first time around. And then, anger had filled the emptiness. Flynn loved to draw, to envision, to create. His misplaced loyalty to his family had robbed him of that joy. Why did he insist on denying his gift? It wasn't as if his selfish mother appreciated his sacrifice, and his father—

"What do you think?" he asked in a rough, groggy, sexier-than-sin voice.

Her pulse sprinted. She studied his beard-stubbled, sleepy-eyed face. It would be so easy to love him again. But she couldn't.

"It's beautiful."

"We can do it, Renee—have our home and family the way we once planned."

The strength of yearning for what he offered scared her so badly she grasped for mental and physical distance. "Why did you do it, Flynn?"

He eased upright in a slow flexing of muscles. "Do what?"

"Give up your dream."

He rose and towered over her, scowling. "We've been over this before."

"It pains me to see you deny your talent with a number-crunching job. I understood when you stepped in during the crisis. Your family needed you. But what about now? The crisis is over. Why can't Brock hire another VP and let you return to your dream job?"

His frown deepened. "It's not as simple as that."

"It could be."

"I never finished my internship."

"It would take less than a year to get all of your certifications."

"I'm not a college kid anymore." Shoulders tight, he headed toward the stairs.

"Denying your passion for architecture won't bring your father back, Flynn," she called after him.

He flinched as if she'd hit him, then pivoted abruptly and charged back toward her, stopping only inches away. He glared down at her. "Why do you care?"

Good question. Why did his happiness matter when she planned to get as far away from him as possible as soon as she had what she wanted from him?

The wall blocking what she'd been trying to deny shattered like glass. She realized it mattered because she was still in love with her husband.

Mentally reeling, she tried to find a safe response. "I don't want my child raised by a bitter, unhappy parent."

"I'm not your mother."

She winced at the accuracy of his barb. "No. You're not."

I won't let myself be, either.

But like Flynn had said, it wasn't as simple as wishing and making it so. Avoiding her mother's mistakes would take constant vigilance.

"I'm going to finish painting." She left him because she was very afraid he'd guess her secrets.

Renee stared up at Gretchen Mahoney's Knob Hill home late Sunday morning. While she admired the ornate architecture and beauty of the exquisitely maintained house, she had no desire to live in such formal surroundings.

This was the type of house Carol Maddox wanted her son to occupy. Instead, Flynn had chosen a diamond-in-the-rough residence and an even less polished wife. Two strikes against Renee in Carol's book.

Renee rang the bell and braced herself to face Flynn's

"friend" who had insisted on a Sunday-morning interview. Despite Renee's questions, Flynn had refused to share any more details about his relationship with the woman. Perhaps she was an acquaintance of his mother who lived in the same posh neighborhood, or a client he knew through work. Maybe she was the wife of an old friend.

The front door opened, revealing a gorgeous, willowy thirty-something brunette in four-inch heels and the kind of designer-chic suit that graced *Vogue* magazine covers. She looked Renee up and down with curiosity-filled olive-green eyes framed by sleek curtains of hair. "You must be Flynn's wife. I'm Gretchen. Come in."

Renee's fingers tightened on her leather portfolio as uneasiness swarmed down her spine and buzzed in the pit of her stomach like a hive of angry bees. "Yes, I'm Renee Maddox."

"According to Flynn, you are exactly what I need for my little soiree." Gretchen led Renee through an immense black-and-white, marble-tiled foyer with a massive staircase and an equally sizable floral arrangement to a formal living room filled with antique furniture and more expensive bouquets.

"Please have a seat." Her hostess flicked a hand toward a white French provincial chair—a ringless left hand. Not the wife of an acquaintance, then.

Was this woman Flynn's lover? Renee sat and tried to focus on the job ahead, but not knowing exactly who Gretchen was or what she was to Flynn made concentrating difficult.

She opened her notebook. "Flynn didn't tell me what kind of event you needed catered. What did you have in mind?"

"Getting right to business, are we? No chitchat?"

Renee blinked. Usually clients with this kind of wealth didn't want to mingle with the lowly help. "I'm sorry. I understood this was a rush job and that you were eager to nail down the details."

"It is and I am. My usual caterer had a heart attack last week and is unable to work."

"I'm sorry. That leaves you in a tight spot. Let's begin with the type of event, the mood you'd like to set and then work our way toward budgets."

Perfectly arched black eyebrows hiked. "Aren't you even a little curious about me? I confess I've been quite curious about you."

Renee didn't know whether to admire the woman for her candor or hate her for being beautiful, rich and poised—all the things Renee was not.

"As a prospective client, you have a right to your questions."

"I only have one question. Do you realize how badly you hurt Flynn when you left?"

Renee stiffened at the personal attack. "Perhaps I should qualify that by saying questions pertaining to my résumé."

Radiating protectiveness rather than malice, Gretchen leaned back in her chair and crossed her endlessly long legs. "Did you ever consider the gossip he'd face after you disappeared? The explanations he'd have to make?"

The woman's audacity amazed Renee. But Gretchen did have a point. After Renee had fled to L.A., she'd tried not to think about Flynn or the mess she'd left behind. She'd thrown herself into a new job and into caring for her grandmother, trying to exhaust herself each day so she could sleep at night—without the booze to help her relax. She'd firmly believed Flynn would be better off without her than with a wife who would become a liability, and she still adhered to that opinion.

"Flynn isn't the make-excuses type." Determined to get this meeting back on a business footing, she clicked her pen. "Do you have a preferred theme for your event?"

"Reputation is everything in advertising. You damaged Flynn's," Gretchen insisted, ignoring Renee's question.

"Ms. Mahoney, could we please stick with business? Unless your party was only a ruse to get me here and harass me, my personal life is really not relative to the service I offer."

"If you believe that, then you're sadly mistaken. In this competitive market, it's not just what you do, but who you know and who you've pleased or crossed in the past. But we'll play this your way. For now."

She slid an embossed invitation across the table. "As you can see I'm hosting a silent auction in my home to raise money for the local women's shelter. The shelter is a place near and dear to my heart."

"It's a worthy cause."

"My second husband rescued me from there."

Surprised, Renee didn't know what to say. Gretchen didn't look like the typical victim of abuse Renee had in her head.

"Once I found the courage to quit hiding my bruises and admit I had a problem, I escaped from my first husband with the help of friends I could count on. Flynn was one of those friends. He's a wonderful man. Supportive. Understanding. I would have married him in an instant—after my second husband died, that is. But a part of Flynn would never have been mine. That part still belongs to you."

Renee's heart stalled and her hand froze, pen clutched above paper. "You're mistaken."

"There are few things in life that I won't share, but my man tops that list."

Alarm skittered down Renee's spine. "Are you warning me off?"

"No. I'm advising you not to hurt Flynn again. He deserves better."

"Better meaning you?"

"Better meaning a woman who is strong enough to honor her commitment to him and not run when the going gets tough."

Anger and shame blended inside Renee. By running away without giving an explanation, she'd left the door open for everyone to think badly of her. She'd thought it better to let people assume the worst, rather than stay, become a drunk and confirm it. She hadn't considered her departure might cast Flynn in a negative light.

With hindsight she realized what she considered an act of self*less*ness could be construed as one of self*ish*ness by others. But admitting that to her hostess would be like handing a possible rival ammunition.

"You're judging me based on something of which you have no knowledge."

"I'm not judging you at all, Renee. I'm merely letting you know I'll be watching. All of Flynn's friends will be. And if you hurt him again, you'll find it very difficult to make a success of your catering business in San Francisco."

After delivering her threat, Gretchen uncrossed her legs and sat forward, the enmity in her eyes changing to excitement. "Now, about my little get-together, I have sixty of San Francisco's wealthiest citizens confirmed for this Friday night. I want them feeling happy and generous. What do you suggest?"

Head reeling at the about-face, Renee mentally adjusted from defense to offense. She wanted to tell Ms. Mahoney to stuff her party right up her designer-clad behind. But she couldn't. She had a business to market, and she couldn't afford to let a verbal skirmish throw her off her game.

But her confrontation with Gretchen made one thing very clear. She had two choices. One: give up on the baby and expansion ideas and retreat before loving Flynn destroyed her. Two: she could fight her demons, charge ahead and try to win back her husband and the life they'd once dreamed of sharing.

From her perspective either choice could be potentially disastrous, but only one offered a reward.

She studied the beautiful, poised woman in front of her. If Gretchen had taken back her life and refused to be a victim, could Renee be any less courageous?

No. She'd kept her drinking issue under control since that turning-point night, and she would continue to do so. Flynn would never have to know.

Ten

Juggling three bags of groceries containing the ingredients for a special dinner consisting of Flynn's favorites, Renee climbed the front steps to the Victorian with a signed contract and a sizable deposit for her first San Francisco event in the leather portfolio swinging from her shoulder.

Deciding to try to rebuild the relationship she'd once shared with Flynn had filled her with energy that not even two stressful hours of planning a short-notice event could take away. During her time with her client, Renee had been forced to admit she wouldn't blame Flynn if he'd had an intimate relationship with the woman after his wife had left him.

Gretchen was smart, creative and, apparently, wielded a lot of clout in the wealthy social circles. She was the type of woman Carol Maddox had wanted her son to marry, and not just because of Gretchen's deceased husband's extreme wealth, but because Gretchen had been born into the same social stratum. With women like that waiting in the wings, Renee knew she had to act now.

Despite the competition, she was looking forward to Friday, to working Gretchen's party and proving to San Francisco's snobs that California Girl's Catering had the right stuff.

Renee let herself in the front door and pocketed her keys. Splatters of red on the floor stopped her. A trail of rose petals led up the staircase.

Her heart pumped harder, making her almost light-headed with excitement. The Flynn she'd fallen in love with had made another appearance. God, she'd missed him and missed having someone to play with, to talk to and plan with. With sudden clarity she realized that's why her attempts to find Mr. Right had failed. None of her dates had understood her the way Flynn had. He got her need to create with food because he shared the same need, only his method of expression was blueprints. Each of them relished seeing something go from an abstract idea to concrete reality.

Despite everything, could the rose petals mean he still cared? Flynn had claimed he wanted her to stay, but he hadn't said he loved her.

Impatient to discover the answer, she dumped the groceries and her briefcase on the credenza and then followed the petal-strewn path. Her body hummed with anticipation. What would she find at the top of those stairs?

Similar incidents from the past rushed forward, crowding her brain with a smorgasbord of happy, sexy, tender and delicious memories of the claw-foot tub with bubbles and petals floating on the surface and Flynn waiting to be her personal bath attendant, a sexy new black cocktail dress with sinful matching lingerie and dancing shoes and Flynn struggling with the bow tie of his tux as he exited the bathroom. Or maybe she'd find Flynn, naked and hungry for her in their bed.

Scratch that thought. The roses turned away from the master suite and led to the closed door of the guest room—her room. Was he waiting in her bed?

"Flynn?"

"In here."

She pushed open her door. The ruby-speckled path led to Flynn, seated by the French doors on the only piece of furniture remaining in the room. Even the rugs had been stripped from the polished hardwood floors. He rose and stepped aside, revealing a wooden rocking chair.

"You'll need this when the baby arrives." He curved his fingers over the high back and stroked the smooth wood. "The man who made the baby furniture made this."

"Where is everything else?" She waved a hand to indicate the empty room.

"I moved your clothes to our room and the bedroom suite upstairs."

A big step, but she was okay with that. "By yourself?"

"Brock helped."

When she'd discovered the roses, she'd expected seduction and sex. Hot, steamy sex. Instead, Flynn had given her something better—a concrete visual of the future within their grasp.

He thumped a knuckle on the hand-carved back of the rocker. "Try it out."

She crossed the room and sank into the chair. The wood, retaining the warmth of Flynn's body, embraced her. Her fingers stroked the glossy armrests. This was where she'd sit and nurse their baby, where she'd rock her son or daughter to sleep. A rush of emotion squeezed her chest.

"It's beautiful, Flynn. I love it. Thank you."

His lips brushed the top of her head, then he circled and knelt in front of her. "Happy Valentine's Day."

Her breath caught. "I forgot all about the holiday. I'm sorry, I didn't get you anything."

"You're here where you belong. That's all I need." He pulled her from the chair and into his arms. His mouth teased hers tenderly at first and then with intensifying passion that made her blood race.

Yes, she was where she belonged. And she would make their marriage work this time. A bond was only as strong as its weakest link, and she would not be that weak link. She would be strong for Flynn and for their baby.

Flynn felt Renee's capitulation clear down to his bones. Her lips moved with his, her supple body melted against him, and her nails dug into his waist, pulling him closer.

Adrenaline shot through him. He'd won.

He wanted to celebrate his success in an act of making love that had nothing to do with making a baby. He swept her into his arms and carried her down the hall. Without breaking the kiss, he laid her in the center of the bed and followed her down.

Her arms slid from his neck to his chest. She tugged at his shirt as if eager to be skin to skin with him—the way she used to. But something was different. There was an urgency to her frantic movements that went beyond hunger.

She hiked his shirttail, slid her hands beneath the fabric and went straight for his erogenous zones, tracing the underside of his arms, along his rib cage, the small of his back, his hipbones. He sucked in a sharp breath when her fingertips dipped into his waistband and hunger overrode his curiosity.

He shrugged off his shirt and then swept her sweater over her head. Her nipples showed clearly through the lace of her white bra. Propping himself on an elbow, he bent and captured one peachy tip. Her scent filled his lungs and the lace abraded his tongue. He raked her puckered flesh with his teeth, tugging gently then sucking. She rewarded him with a soft "Mmm."

She cradled his head with one hand. The other worked the button and zipper of his khaki pants, and then she slid her hand inside his open fly, cupping, then stroking his erection. Desire pulsed through him, making him harder, hotter and impatient to sink into her wetness.

He rolled away from her talented hands, knelt and quickly stripped her skirt down her legs. He paused long enough to admire her white bikini panties and then those and her bra had to go, leaving her in nothing but glistening golden curls and her black heels.

Like a cat, she rolled into a kneeling position and reached for him. He evaded her grasp long enough to stand by the side of the bed and shuck the remainder of his clothing under her hungry gaze. Her palms splayed on her thighs and her full breasts called for attention. Blue-violet eyes scrolled over him and she licked her lips. His pulse rate doubled.

Why had no other woman ever affected him as strongly as Renee did? And how the hell could Renee have walked away from this as if it didn't matter? As if *he* didn't matter.

"Make love with me, Flynn. I need you. Here." Her

husky whisper followed by her fingers gliding down her torso, combing through her curls and covering what he yearned for demolished his anger and any chance he had of taking it slow.

He craved the taste of her. Lunging forward, he feasted on her mouth, her neck, her breasts, belly and navel, then finally reached her nectar. No one tasted like Renee, and no one other than her had been able to satisfy his need.

He licked, sucked and nibbled her until her cries filled his ears and her spasming body arched off the bed. He wanted to be unselfish, to bring her to orgasm multiple times, but he had to be inside her. *Now.* Palming her bottom, he lifted her. Her fingers curled around his erection, stroking him, then guiding him. He slid into her wet, welcoming warmth, and his muscles locked as he fought for control and savored the feel of her.

Her internal muscles gripped him and her fingers, digging into his butt, urged him to move. He couldn't resist. He pumped harder and faster, her slickness coaxing his way.

Her hands rushed over his body, as if urgently mapping his muscles, then her nails skimmed his nipples. Jaw-clenching bolts of pleasure shot through him. He tried to focus on her, on her soft gasps, on the jiggle of her full breasts with each hard thrust, on finding and caressing her center.

He lost it. His climax exploded, sending shards of ecstasy through his body.

One corner of his mind registered Renee's cries as she joined him, and along with repletion, the sense of coming home, of finally being where he belonged, overwhelmed him.

Lungs bellowing, he eased down beside her. Not knowing the reason she'd left the first time meant he couldn't prevent her leaving again. The lack of control unsettled him.

Then he rolled onto his back and stared at the ceiling. Renee shifted, hooking her thigh over his and her arm over his torso. She'd always been a snuggler. He held her close, savoring the melding of their damp bodies. He should have gotten over her. Any self-respecting man would have. And he had tried. But Renee was the only person he'd ever known who'd understood his need to create and encouraged him to follow his dream of becoming an architect when even his family cursed his choice.

Her fingers walked a path up his abdomen to his chest. She drew a shape over his left pectoral. A heart. Another blast from the past. They used to write messages on each other's skin.

"I love you, Flynn. I always have."

Her breathless declaration sent his heart slamming into his ribs beneath her hand. He turned his head, met her gaze and saw her words reflected in her gaze. He wanted to believe her, but doubts nagged at him. "Then why did you leave?"

Tension invaded her muscles and her fist clenched on his chest. Her eyes turned evasive, long lashes descending to shield her thoughts. "I didn't want to. But I had to. Please, *please* believe I thought my getting out of your life was the best thing for everyone concerned."

He couldn't blindly believe without facts. Not this time. "What happened, Renee?"

She pulled away, tugging the edge of the comforter with her as she climbed from the bed. "I—I had to go, okay? That's all I can say."

"Was there someone else?" He voiced the words that had been lurking in his subconscious—words he'd been trying to ignore.

Her shock appeared genuine. "No. Oh, no. Never. I loved you. Only you, Flynn."

He rose and faced her across the mattress. "I need more of an explanation than that."

She bit her lip. "You'll have to take my word for it. I love you, and I'll love our baby…if there is one."

"And if there isn't?"

"You said yourself we'd keep trying. I want to be with you, Flynn. I want everything we once planned. The family, the house, the fenced yard, the dog. All of it. And I want it with you. But you have to trust me."

Trust her. She had no idea how much she was asking. He'd counted on her before and she'd let him down. Did he dare risk making the same mistake twice?

High on satisfaction, Renee hummed a tune as she packed up her cooking utensils in Gretchen's kitchen Friday night.

The week with Flynn had been just short of heavenly. The nursery was perfect with its new furniture and pale mint paint. CGC's new quarters were finished and beautiful. And life with Flynn…

Renee wanted to do a happy dance. Their relationship was almost back to where it had been before his father died. He hadn't said he loved her yet, but there had been tenderness in his eyes and in every gesture. That had to mean something.

She lifted the box of utensils, noting as the edge pressed against her that her breasts were tender. Her pulse quickened. Was she pregnant? Or was the soreness a symptom of her monthly visitor, which was due any day now? Was it too soon to do a pregnancy test?

Eager to get home to Flynn and tell him how well CGC's entry into the San Francisco market had gone, she set the box of her belongings down near the servants' entrance and glanced at her watch. The event should be over in a matter of minutes. Tack on clean-up time and she should be home around one. She hoped Flynn would be up.

The kitchen door swung open. Mindy, one of Renee's three temporary workers, rushed in. Her tuxedo-skirt ensemble still looked as fresh as it had when she'd started her shift three hours ago, but the woman looked frazzled.

Mindy set the serving tray on the counter. "Red wine spill on the living room rug."

"I'll get it." Renee jumped into action, grabbing a bottle of club soda and a rag. She'd spent the entire evening in the kitchen preparing food and refilling trays. She seized the opportunity to do a walk-through and made her way toward the designated area.

Only a dozen or so of the expensively dressed and perfumed guests lingered, most of whom had spilled out the open doors on the far side of the room and into the conservatory. A massive flower arrangement on the top of the closed grand piano partially obscured Renee's view.

She spotted the stain and knelt. The club soda fizzled as she poured, diluting the red wine and bringing it to the surface of the expensive Aubusson carpet. She blotted and repeated the procedure.

"You simply must tell me how you managed to find a caterer of this caliber at the last minute," a familiar voice said, stopping Renee mid-blot.

Flynn's mother was here. Renee grimaced. Dislike

curdled in her stomach, overshadowing the compliment. Facing the witch would kill the buzz of a successful night.

"Carol, you know I never divulge my secrets," Gretchen replied.

The women paused on the opposite side of the piano just inside the open doors. The only parts of them Renee could see from her position were their thousand-dollar shoes and legs below the hems of their cocktail dresses. That meant they couldn't see her, either.

"I must hire him for my next event. The food and presentation were absolutely superb," Carol continued.

Pride filled Renee's chest. The menu she and Gretchen had chosen had turned out exquisitely, if she did say so herself.

"I'll pass on your compliments," Gretchen replied.

"You might as well stop playing games. You know I'll find out who you used. I have my ways." Carol's tone sounded more threatening than teasing.

"You are extremely well-connected, and if my caterer wishes to make your acquaintance, I'll give her your contact information and let her get in touch."

Renee debated staying hidden while she blotted up the last of the spill, but skulking behind furniture to avoid unpleasant people wasn't her way. Not anymore. Seven years ago it would have been—a fact Carol Maddox had used to her advantage.

On the other hand, Renee owed Gretchen her loyalty for taking a chance on her, but building her business would be impossible if she didn't get her name out.

The expensive heels moved in her direction, taking the decision out of her hands. She would not be on her knees in front of her mother-in-law. She rose. "Good evening, Carol."

Her mother-in-law's shocked eyes fixed on Renee like laser beams. Despite Carol's chemically paralyzed face, her distaste couldn't be clearer. She took in Renee's crisp white chef's uniform and her lip actually twitched in a sneer. "Hired help now, are you?"

Renee bit the inside of her lip on the waspish comment that came to mind. She wouldn't stoop to Carol's level. "Yes. I'm the help you're so desperate to identify. I catered the party tonight. Thank you for your compliments."

She reached into her pocket and withdrew a newly printed business card and offered it to her mother-in-law.

Carol lifted her chin, turned on her heel and stalked away—without the card.

"Why does her rudeness not surprise me?" Renee asked rhetorically.

"She is a witch," Gretchen confirmed. "But she's an influential one. Getting on her bad side isn't a good idea."

"I've been on Carol's hate list since the day Flynn brought me home to meet the family eight and a half years ago."

Gretchen made a sympathetic moue. "The only reason I'm not on the same list is because my family could buy and sell her ten times over, and since I now control all that lovely money..." She shrugged and glanced over her shoulder. "Let me share a little something I learned from being an abused wife. People can only make you feel inferior if you let them."

Renee identified the paraphrased quote. "Eleanor Roosevelt."

"Yes. I've learned to hold my head high—especially when the sharks are circling in the water. And make no mistake about it, Carol Maddox is a shark. If she smells blood in the water, she will attack from your weakest side, and she won't be particularly concerned about collateral damage."

A frisson raced over Renee, but Gretchen wasn't telling her anything she didn't already know. "I'll keep that in mind."

But she wasn't going to let Carol's snobbery dampen her good mood. Instead, Renee planned to focus on her successes and her future with Flynn.

"You exceeded my expectations for tonight, Renee. I enjoyed working with you, and you literally saved my event, and because of that I raised a lot of cash for the shelter. Leave as many business cards as you brought with you. I'll see that they end up in the right hands." With a nod, Gretchen returned to her guests.

Renee smiled. Apart from her mother-in-law, life was just about perfect right now, and Renee wasn't going to let anything or anyone ruin it for her this time, not even Carol Maddox.

Renee stuffed the party leftovers in the refrigerator and closed the door.

Bedtime.

It was just after one in the morning and she should be exhausted, but she was still too keyed up to sleep.

She couldn't help feeling a teensy bit deflated. She wanted to share her excitement with Flynn, but the lights had been off upstairs when she'd pulled into the driveway fifteen minutes ago, which meant Flynn was probably asleep. But mostly, she'd wanted to thank him for making tonight happen with his calls to Gretchen and the employment agency.

She crossed to the laundry room, stripped off her uniform and dropped it into the washer. Rolling her tense shoulders, she returned to the kitchen and jerked to a stop. Flynn waited with one hip parked against the counter. He wore nothing but his boxers.

She took in his gorgeous physique and her mouth watered. "Did I wake you?"

His eyes raked her nakedness. "Trust me, even if you had, the view is well worth the trip downstairs. I was waiting for you. I wanted to hear about your night."

She grinned. "The event went well. I have leftovers in the fridge if you're hungry."

"Maybe later. I have other plans for you."

The glint in his eyes made her heart trip. "Care to elaborate?"

"Come upstairs and find out." He extended his hand.

Desire coiled inside her belly as she laid her palm across his. Flynn jerked her close. Their bodies slapped together. He pressed a quick hard kiss on her lips and then drew back. Looking her up and down, hunger evident in his eyes and in the bulge rising in his briefs, he shook his head as if denying himself and then led her upstairs.

"Flynn, thank you for tonight," she said as she climbed. "None of this would have happened if you hadn't called Gretchen."

"You're welcome."

When she reached the landing she heard water running. In the bedroom she smelled her favorite bath salts. And then in the bathroom, she spotted the steaming claw-foot tub.

Flynn's hands landed on her shoulders. He pulled her back flush against his front. "Just as I expected. Your muscles are knotted. Nights on the town always jazzed you up before. I thought you might need to unwind. Remember how we used to end most party nights in here?"

The memories of sexy shared baths combined with his teeth grazing the curve of her shoulder made her shiver. "Yes. Does that mean you're going to join me?"

She felt his smile against her neck. "Not this time. You soak and give me a replay of the night. I'll play masseur and enjoy the view."

She tested the water and then climbed into the tub. Flynn lathered his hands and then sat on a vanity stool he'd placed behind her head. He gently dug his thumbs into her tense neck muscles, rubbing out the kinks until she sighed.

"That feels wonderful."

"Relax." He pressed a kiss on her ear and kneaded her shoulders. "I hope tonight is just the beginning of a new successful venture, but if it takes a while to get CGC off the ground, that's okay. There's nothing we can't handle if you level with me."

She knew he still wondered why she'd run seven years ago. She'd caught him watching her with a question in his eyes several times. She yearned to confess. But she said nothing. Flynn hated weakness as much as she did. He'd once claimed he'd stand by her, and he would because he was an honorable guy. But he'd lose respect for her if he learned the truth. She couldn't bear watching his love die again. The first time had nearly destroyed her.

Eleven

Flynn caught himself sketching on his blotter again Monday afternoon—this time a miniature version of the Victorian complete with a lookout tower turret—a fort/playhouse for his and Renee's children.

Children. He didn't even know if she was pregnant yet and he was already thinking in multiples. He found her confident, ambitious persona far sexier than her younger, eager-to-please version had been.

He raked a hand over his jaw and tried to refocus on the columns of numbers in front of him, but Madd Comm's rivalry with Golden Gate Promotions couldn't hold his attention.

Since Renee's return he'd had a hard time maintaining his interest in the Maddox bottom line. His mind flicked back to Friday night. When he'd heard Renee's van enter the driveway after Gretchen's party, he hadn't been able to wait for her to come upstairs. He'd wanted to share her enthusiasm—or her disappointment. The bath he'd run for her had ended with a hot make-out session followed by leftover hors d'oeuvres eaten in bed while she told him about the event.

The fire of excitement in her eyes while she'd talked had reminded him of the woman he'd fallen in love with so long ago and of what he'd stripped from her the first time around. Asking her to live without a creative outlet was the same as asking her to live without air. He knew that now. No wonder she'd left him.

Like him, Renee needed to feel pride in her accomplishments. By making her a homebody, he'd limited her outlets.

His door burst open and his brother stormed in. "Have you seen this?"

Brock held a newspaper opened to the society, aka gossip, page.

"I don't read that crap. I'm surprised you do."

"Shelby brought it to my attention. You might reconsider reading it since you, your wife and Maddox Communications are mentioned."

Flynn's senses went on red alert. "Judging by your tone, I take it the article isn't a positive recap of Renee's Friday-night catering job."

"Far from it."

Flynn took the paper and skimmed the page looking for what had sent Brock into orbit.

Ad Agency's Top Gun Shoots Blanks?

The headline hit him like a sucker punch. He gritted his teeth and read on.

What's a thirty-something woman to do when her biological clock starts ticking and she can't find suitable daddy material? Renee Landers Maddox, wife of Flynn Maddox, VP of Maddox Communications, reportedly took matters into her own hands recently and visited a local sperm bank. Rumor has it she petitioned for a deposit made by her estranged husband, but that deposit was destroyed. Now she and hubby claim to be reconciling. Meanwhile she has launched a branch of her catering business in L.A. out of his Pacific Heights basement.

Is this a case of home-is-where-the-heart-is or just a form of direct deposit? If Maddox's VP is faking his marriage, what else is he faking? Stay tuned. But I wouldn't suggest hiring California Girl's Catering with a party date of nine months from now, since Mr. and Mrs. Maddox have already purchased nursery furniture.

Flynn wanted to rip the gossip rag to shreds. But that wouldn't solve the problem. "Renee doesn't need this when she's trying to get CGC off the ground."

"Is it true? She tried to get your sperm bank deposit?"

"That is nobody's business but ours, Brock."

"It's my business if it affects Maddox Communications. And that column slanders Maddox Communications, too."

"Who in the hell would make a personal attack like this?"

"I only know one person who stands to gain if Maddox looks shady, and he happens to fight dirty."

Flynn didn't need a genius IQ to follow Brock's line of thought. "Athos Koteas? But why target Renee?"

"Because she's your weak spot. You didn't answer my question. Is your reconciliation a sham? Is she back just for a kid?"

He owed his brother the truth. "Our reunion started out that way when the clinic contacted me about Renee requesting my sample. That's why I asked about the divorce papers, and then I subsequently found out we were still married. Renee agreed to move back in if I'd father her child. But our marriage isn't a pretense anymore."

Brock cursed and strode to the window. "How many people knew about that stupid college prank?"

"Only family and the other fraternity guys involved, but they made deposits, too. Outing me would also bring their parts in the stupid bet to light." Flynn tapped his pen on his blotter. "If we have a leak in the office, the perpetrator could have gotten the info from my office. The sperm bank faxed forms to me here. I kept copies just in case something went wrong."

Brock cursed. "There is no 'if' we have a spy. Someone at Maddox is feeding proprietary information to Koteas."

"If it is Koteas." Flynn didn't know why Renee had left him the first time. Would this embarrassment be enough to send her running again? He had to fix this before that happened. But how? "I don't want Renee to find out about this."

Brock pivoted, his mouth agape. "It's a paper with a circulation of tens of thousands. You can't buy and burn every copy or keep people who've already read the column from talking."

"I need to get Renee out of town until the scandal blows over. No. Scratch that. She'll want to be here to take calls and make appointments for CGC."

"You could try to get the rag to print a retraction."

Flynn scanned the damning words again. They didn't sound any better the second time. "Technically, nothing they've printed is untrue."

The intercom on his desk buzzed. "A reporter from the *San Francisco Journal* is on line one," Cammie said. "He wants to ask you about a sperm bank?"

Reporters. Damn. "Hold all my calls. And, Cammie, don't talk to any reporters. I'm going out."

"Now?" Brock asked.

Flynn scrubbed his knotting neck muscles and rose. "I'm going to talk to Koteas. If I leave now he may still be in his office."

"What good will talking to that bastard do?"

"I don't know, but I have to do something. Or I might lose Renee again."

"Lay off my wife," Flynn growled at Athos Koteas across the man's wide desk.

The seventy-year-old founder of Golden Gate Promotions laid down the paper Flynn had thrust at him, leaned back in his massive leather chair and cracked an amused smile.

"Aah. Children. They are both a blessing and a curse. We have such high hopes for them when they are born. But my three sons—" he shook his head "—they are useless. You, on the other hand, have no interest in advertising, but like a good son, you joined your father's firm when duty called."

That duty had cost him his marriage, and then Flynn

realized Koteas knew too much about him. But that wasn't why Flynn was here. He was here because the damned reporter had refused to divulge her source when Flynn had called on his way to Golden Gate's offices. He'd had to go with his original suspect.

"Why target my wife?"

"As much as I would like to take credit for that interesting tale, I cannot. I do not waste my time on tabloids."

Flynn studied the man's heavily lined face and steady dark eyes and found no evidence that Koteas lied. "No one else stands to gain from this story."

"Are you sure? Think harder, Mr. Maddox. Everyone has enemies, including your lovely wife."

Who could dislike Renee?

"Good luck finding the viper in your nest," Koteas added.

In your nest.

Flynn clenched his teeth as his thoughts raced ahead. He had a suspicion who that poisonous snake might be. Someone who had made Renee's life difficult since the day Flynn had first brought her home.

His mother.

She wasn't pregnant.

Renee's knees buckled under the weight of disappointment. She sank into the new rocking chair and pushed off with her toe. But the repetitive back-and-forth motion didn't soothe her. She'd come so close to having everything she'd once dreamed of with Flynn.

She wanted him here, wanted his arms around her and his assurances that they could try again. Her need for him was stupid really. She was used to standing on her own feet. But she needed a sympathetic shoulder, and he was the only one who would understand and be as disappointed as she was over the negative pregnancy test.

She pulled her cell phone from her pocket and dialed his private work number. Voice mail picked up. She hung up and tried his assistant's number. "Flynn Maddox's office, Cammie speaking. How may I help you?"

"Cammie, it's Renee. I need to talk to Flynn."

"Hello, Renee. Flynn's out. I'm not sure if he'll be back today. May I take a message?"

This wasn't news he needed to hear secondhand. "No. I'll call his cell phone."

She disconnected and dialed his cell. No answer. She tried again and still received no response. She checked the new teddy-bear clock on the nursery wall. Almost five. He should be home soon.

Until then, she would hang tight and wait. The flashback to the past and waiting for Flynn to come home kinked her muscles. But this time was different. She wouldn't turn to the bottle.

She was stronger now. She had too much to lose. And she'd learned her lesson.

Hadn't she?

"What in the hell were you thinking?" Flynn asked his mother Monday evening in the living room of her lavish Knob Hill house.

She broke eye contact and fussed with her diamond earring. "You have no proof I spoke to that reporter."

"You knew about my college prank. You dislike Renee, and your driver took you to meet the reporter at Chez Mari Saturday afternoon. How much more proof do I need?"

His mother's taxidermy-tight face blanched. "Renee Landers is not good enough for you."

Anger roared through him like a canyon fire. "Maddox, mother. Renee Maddox." He enjoyed her flinch. "She's the woman I married and the one who will be having your grandchildren. That's all that matters."

"What matters is that you end this marriage before she gets her hooks into you by tying you down with her low-class, white-trash brats. I only spoke to the columnist because I wanted Renee to leave. I had hoped she'd realize she's an embarrassment and a liability to you and Madd—"

His teeth slammed together. How had he missed this vicious enmity before? "Renee is not an embarrassment or a liability. She is the only person who puts my happiness above her own."

And that had always been the case, which made her leaving seven years ago all that much more intriguing. Had she left out of some misguided belief he'd be better off without her?

"You're wrong, Flynn. I want you to be happy, and finding a suitable wife will make you happy."

"As happy as your marriage made you?"

His mother's chin jerked up. "I don't know what you mean."

"Did you ever love my father? If you did I never saw signs of it. You tolerated him because he bankrolled your spending habits. You gave him children not because of any maternal urge, but only because it was expected of you, and children guaranteed Dad would continue supporting you financially."

"That's not true."

He didn't bother to argue. He knew the facts. The

memories of growing up in a cold, unloving household were too vivid to forget. No wonder his father had spent all his time at the office.

Flynn hadn't known love until Renee had chiseled down his walls and forced her way into his heart with her humor, intelligence and generosity.

"Think very carefully before you make your choice, Mother."

"What are you saying?"

"Either you apologize to Renee, or you say goodbye to me. I'll walk out that door and we're through."

"Don't be ridiculous, Flynn. I'm your mother."

"A fact that brings me nothing but shame at the moment. I knew you were unhappy, but I didn't realize you'd become a bitter, vindictive old woman."

Ignoring her gasp, he turned on his heel and stormed out of the house. He needed his wife. Only Renee's kisses could heal the wound of dealing with a parent who would stab him in the back.

Eight o'clock. Flynn was late.

Renee stared at the kitchen counters laden with cookies, a pie and quiche. She'd needed a way to deal with her agitation—an outlet other than drinking.

Flynn hadn't called and his cell phone dumped straight to voice mail. The hospitals had no reports of anyone matching his description being brought in. She knew. She'd called all the local emergency rooms. Twice. Her stomach burned from nerves.

She had to admit Flynn's well-stocked liquor cabinet was tempting. Drinking herself into oblivion and not having to worry would certainly be easier than concocting new recipes and walking the floor. But she resisted.

She wasn't her mother. She'd developed better coping skills for dealing with her problems than numbing them out. She cooked. She cleaned. If all else failed she read cooking magazines online.

She heard a key turn in the front door and her pulse jumped like a runner hearing the starter's pistol. Wiping her hands on a towel, she raced down the hall and reached the foyer as Flynn entered. Anger combined with worry and grief tangled inside her. She wanted to scream at him for scaring her and throw herself into his arms and cry in relief because he was okay.

"Where have you been?"

He frowned at her frantic tone. "Has anyone called?"

She stared at him in disbelief. "No. Not even you. You're hours late. Answer my question, Flynn."

Silently he withdrew a folded newspaper from his briefcase. Confused, she took it from him. He pointed at a headline halfway down the page.

Ad Agency's Top Gun Shoots Blanks?

Uneasiness swirled through her like a cold, damp fog. Her heart inched up her throat as she read the rest of the article. Someone had used her to attack Flynn and Maddox Communications. Flynn had said reputation was everything, and this article wasn't helping his.

"Who would do this?"

He wiped a hand over his face. Only then did she notice his tightly clenched jaw and the lines of stress bracketing his mouth. "I spent the afternoon trying to find out. Brock and I suspected Athos Koteas, Maddox's rival. But it wasn't him."

"Then who?"

"My mother."

Reeling, Renee staggered into the den and collapsed on the sofa. "Does she hate me so badly that to get to me she'd hurt you and malign the company that pays her bills?"

"I'm sorry, Renee. My mother has always been difficult, but I had no idea she'd stoop so low."

Feeling sick to her stomach, Renee gulped. She'd never had anyone treat her so viciously and had no idea how to react. Maybe she should call her mother. Lorraine had never been one for giving advice, but most of her mother's relationships ended with the same kind of brutal emotional battles. Lorraine would know how to deal with this situation.

Never mind. Lorraine's way of coping would be to ingest large quantities of booze until she forgot. Renee wasn't interested in that kind of medicine.

But if her mother-in-law would rather humiliate her than admit she was a success, then Renee had to wonder what her child's life would be like with a witch like Carol for a grandmother. No child deserved that.

Renee rose and paced to the window.

She loved Flynn, but the sperm bank wasn't the most appalling part of her past. She couldn't risk someone digging up the sordid details and hurting him even more. She had no choice. To take the heat off him and Maddox Communications, she was going to have to leave.

"I can't live in a glass house, Flynn."

"My mother isn't going to cause us any more trouble."

"You can't know that." Her heart ached. She blinked and swallowed the tears burning her eyes and throat. "I'm going back to L.A."

"Good idea. Take a week. By the time you return this will have blown over."

She closed her eyes, took a deep breath and gathered her courage. "I'm not coming back."

He flinched. "What about the baby? What about us?"

She'd been devastated just hours ago, but maybe it was a blessing that she wasn't pregnant. "I did a pregnancy test today. It was negative. I've been trying to call you all afternoon to tell you."

The pain and disappointment on his face wrenched her. "We'll try again."

"I won't raise a family in a verbal war zone. I've been there, Flynn, and I always swore I'd never do that to any child of mine. We need to end this—end *us*."

She couldn't risk repeating her mother's mistakes. This time she'd been strong enough to resist the lure of the alcohol cabinet. Next time she might not have the strength. And what would having a drunk for a wife do for Flynn's reputation? "I'll have my attorney contact yours."

Flynn caught her upper arms. The warmth of his hands penetrated her clothing, but did nothing to warm the cold knot forming inside her. She wanted him to hug her and tell her it would be all right. But she knew it wouldn't. "That's it? You're just going to quit?"

"It's better this way. Trust me." A sob welled up inside her. She mashed her lips together to hold it in. It was because she loved him that she had to let him go.

"Trust you? Apparently, that's the last thing I should do. At the first sign of trouble you run."

Renee flinched, but she didn't explain. Flynn might not enjoy working for Maddox Communications as much as he had the architectural firm, but the VP position was the one he'd chosen, and she had to support him in any way she could. And the best way to help him was to get far away and completely disassociate from him. With her history, having her around would always be a time bomb waiting to explode and damage Maddox's credibility and reputation.

"I'm sorry, Flynn." She brushed past him and raced up the stairs, hoping to reach their room—*his* room—before her tears started falling. She closed and locked the door, then frantically threw the necessities into her suitcases.

When she couldn't stall any longer, she lugged her bags downstairs. Flynn stood stiffly in the den, hands in his pockets, staring out the window into the darkness.

Emotion choked her. She couldn't have spoken even if she'd known what to say, and she didn't.

How did you tell a man you loved him too much to stay?

You didn't.

"I'll send someone for the rest of my stuff."

And then, for the second time, she walked away from the only man she'd ever love.

"Aren't you joining us for Happy Hour at the Rosa?" Brock asked from Flynn's doorway Friday evening.

Flynn looked up from the numbers on his screen—numbers he hadn't really been seeing. His mind had been elsewhere. "No."

Brock entered and closed the door. "It's been four days since Renee left, Flynn. You have to pull yourself out of this funk."

"You're a fine one to talk. You look like hell."

Brock held up his hands. "Hey, don't shoot the messenger. And forget about me. I'll be fine as soon as we catch the Maddox snitch. The team's leaving in five minutes if you change your mind and want to walk down to the bar with us."

Flynn's head wasn't into celebrating the end of another week tonight. "I won't."

"Your loss." Brock reached for the doorknob.

"Brock, I can't do this anymore."

Frowning, Brock paused. "Do what?"

"Crunch numbers."

"You need a vacation? Fine. Take one."

"It's more than that. I'm thinking long-term."

"Flynn, you're not thinking straight. You'll get over Renee and—"

"That's just it. I am thinking straight for the first time in a long time. And if I didn't get over Renee in seven years, then I never will. She said something before she left about living in glass houses. She's right. Madd Comm requires us to live our lives open to others' inspection, commentary and judgment—even if it doesn't make us happy."

"That's because our clients stand to lose a lot of money if we do something that violates their moral code or that of the people who buy their products."

"I'm violating a moral code. Mine. I'm living a lie."

"What are you talking about?"

"I hate this job. I hate crunching numbers and pushing paper. I like designing, building, watching a plan go from a one-dimensional rough sketch on paper to a six-dimensional structure I can walk through, smell and touch. I'm happier slinging paint with Renee than I am inking multimillion-dollar deals for Madd Comm. I still love her."

The realization had hit him like a runaway trolley car when he'd awoken alone in bed this morning. He missed Renee. Her smile, her energy. The way she encouraged him to follow his dreams and loved him even when he didn't. Together they made amazing things happen. Without her he just went through the motions—living without living at all.

"You'll get over this. Trust me. I've been there."

Flynn shook his head. "Renee is right. Working here won't make Dad proud of me or bring him back. I don't want to pretend to enjoy this anymore. It's time to live for me."

"Flynn, don't do anything rash."

"This isn't a rash decision. It's all I've thought about since she left." Flynn turned off his computer and rose with a sense of satisfaction swelling his chest, as if he'd finally gotten something right after he'd been working on it for a very long time. And he had. He'd finally gotten his priorities straight.

"I refuse to give strangers the right to decide how I live my life. I'll have my resignation on your desk Monday morning."

"Take the weekend to think it over."

"There's nothing to think over. I know what I want."

"And what is that exactly?"

"I'm going to finish my architectural internship. I only had six months left when I quit. There will be some remediation, but frankly, even if I have to start over on day one and work through the whole five-year internship again, I'm willing. At least then, if I have to live alone, I'll at least like the company I keep."

"You're out of your mind."

"No, Brock, I'm finally in my right mind. And I have Renee to thank for that." He brushed by his brother on the way out the door.

"Where are you going?" Brock called after him.

"I'm going after my wife."

Twelve

Tamara lingered by the door of Renee's cottage. "Are you sure you don't want to go camping with us this weekend? The girls would love to have you."

Renee shuddered. "Your girls would love to laugh at me. I don't camp. Bugs, snakes and I are not on friendly terms. I'd squeal and scream and, suffice to say, not be a happy camper." Even though she was mentally and physically exhausted and heartbroken, she forced a light tone for her assistant's sake. She'd been faking "fine" all week.

Tamara frowned and bit her lip. "Maybe we could go another weekend."

"Don't you dare cancel on them. Besides, we have events booked for the next four Saturdays."

"But—"

"But nothing. Scram or you're fired."

Tamara stuck out her tongue. "You can't fire me. You don't know the secret ingredient in my salsa recipe."

Renee laughed at their old joke. "No. And I would go out of business without that recipe. Go and have a great time. I'll be fine. I'm going to tweak that carrot cake recipe."

Tamara sighed. "Promise me you won't work all night again."

Renee grimaced. She'd been up late cooking every night this week. The local soup kitchen appreciated her efforts even if her assistant did not. "I promise I'll be in bed before I turn into a pumpkin at midnight."

Her reluctance obvious, Tamara finally left.

Renee scanned her kitchen and her gaze landed on her granny's ladder-back chair. She found comfort in the familiar piece of furniture. It was as if her granny were here to guide her through this rough patch.

Monday, when she had her head together, she'd contact the appliance people about selling the equipment she'd installed in Flynn's basement and try to recoup some of her financial losses. But this week…she just hadn't been able to handle the idea of tearing down what she and Flynn had built together. Not yet.

With that decided, she turned back to her mixer and the notes she'd been making on the cake recipe. When the doorbell rang in what seemed like only a few minutes later, Renee glanced at her watch. *Eight?*

Three hours had passed since Tamara had left. Shouldn't she and the girls be zipped into their sleeping bags or roasting marshmallows by now? But who else would drop by unannounced at this time of night?

Renee wouldn't put it past her assistant to bring the girls and their camping gear here and insist on putting up the tent in the cottage's back garden. Tamara had been hovering ever since she'd shown up for work Tuesday morning and found Renee already busy in the kitchen surrounded by mounds of food.

Renee headed for the front door and caught a glimpse of a taxi driving away through the window. Who would take a taxi to her house? She flicked on the porch light and glanced through the peephole. Flynn stood on her welcome mat.

Heart pounding, she staggered back a step. Why was he here?

She didn't want to see him. She wasn't ready. Panic set in.

A fist pounded on the door. "Renee, I know you're in there. Open up."

Loving him and knowing she couldn't have him hurt more than she could have imagined. But leaving had been for his own good. She had to remember that.

Wiping her damp palms on her jeans, she took a deep breath and opened the door. She drank in the sight of him with his dark hair tousled and five-o'clock shadow darkening his jaw. He looked tired. His tie hung askew and the top button of his white shirt gaped open, as did the coat of his black designer suit.

She looked past him, but his BMW wasn't in the driveway. "Why did you take a taxi?"

"I chartered a plane to get me here faster. Besides, you can't throw me out if I have no way to leave."

His logic startled a laugh from her. "I could just call another cab."

"It would take at least an hour for it to get here. That's an hour I could use to talk some sense into you."

"Sense? Into me?"

"You can't leave me, Renee. I love you."

She gasped. Those were the words she'd longed to hear. But it was too late.

"We're good together, Renee. No one understands me the way you do. No one loves me the way you do." He moved forward and she automatically stepped back and let him in. Dumb move. She should have shut the door in his face.

"Flynn—"

He brushed her cheek with his fingertips and erased whatever protest she'd meant to make. "You love me. Admit it."

She couldn't deny it. "It's not that simple."

How could she make him understand? She turned and led him into the living room.

With a sinking feeling of doom, she realized she'd have to tell him the truth—all of it—and watch his love die. "It was never you, Flynn. It was about me."

He took her hands and pulled her down on the sofa beside him. "Explain."

The love and patience in his eyes tore her apart, but that love wouldn't last long when he learned the truth.

Just do it. Spit it out like ripping off a bandage. Fast.

"After your father died I...I started turning into my mother."

"How?"

She gulped down her fear. "My drinking started innocently enough. I'd open a bottle of wine to share a glass with you when you got home. Then you'd be late. I'd start thinking about what your mother said. How I didn't fit into your crowd. How I was an embarrassment to you when you had to meet with clients, and that I'd never be smart enough to carry my end of a conversation, since I didn't have a college degree. And I'd have a second glass of wine and wonder if Carol was right. Maybe you did regret marrying me. Maybe that was why you didn't want to tie yourself to me with a baby. Maybe there was someone else."

Fury filled his eyes. "My mother said all that?"

Renee nodded.

"Renee, from the day I met you in that paint store there was never another woman. I was working."

"But you weren't coming home."

He wiped his face. Regret filled his eyes. "The adjustment to the VP job wasn't going well. I felt as if I was failing and letting the team down. I was exhausted from trying to clean up the mess my father left behind, and when I came home and you wanted to make love… sometimes I was so exhausted I couldn't. I knew the rejections hurt you, and I hated the idea of failing at home, too, so I slept at the office."

With hindsight, what he said made perfect sense. "I wish you'd told me."

"I didn't want to burden you. Besides my mother's viciousness, what made you leave?"

A fresh wave of shame washed over her. "One day I woke up and there were two empty wine bottles on the floor. I didn't even remember opening the second one. I realized I was becoming my mother. So I ran. I came home to L.A., and Granny helped me find a therapist."

"You should have come to me."

"Why? So I could see you lose respect for me because I was weak? So I could watch your love die? I saw that happen over and over again with my 'uncles' when they discovered my mother was an alcoholic."

"You're saying you're an alcoholic?"

She searched his face, looking for condemnation, and found none. "I don't know, Flynn. I've talked to several counselors. They seem to think that because my drinking only lasted a couple of months and I stopped voluntarily that maybe I'm not. I've worked very hard to develop healthy coping skills for my stress. But I have my mother's genes. I can't take the chance on *maybe,* so I err on the side of caution."

"That's why you don't drink."

She nodded. "I don't want to trigger whatever it is that makes people fall into that downward spiral."

"I think you're too strong to fall."

"Even strong people falter."

He brushed his fingertips over her cheek. "What does that have to do with us not being together for the next fifty years?"

Her love for him swelled inside her. "Flynn, I would never want to force someone I love to become an enabler like my grandmother and I had to be. We had to cover for my mother, make excuses for her. You're better off without me. Not only am I a risk, but my DNA is also contaminated. Our children could carry the tendency to be alcoholics."

"Renee, if only perfect people had children, the population would cease to exist. We'll teach our children those healthy coping skills you mentioned. I love you, and I want you in my life."

Hope fizzed inside her, but she burst the bubble. "I can't live with the idea of others always watching and waiting to pounce on my weakness and use it against you or Maddox Communications."

"You won't have to. I'm leaving Madd Comm."

Surprise stole her breath. "Why?"

"You told me seven and a half years ago that if I couldn't be happy with myself, then I could never be happy with anyone else. And you were right. I finally understand what that means. I was trying to live the life my father had mapped out for me, instead of the one I wanted for myself—the one we had planned with each other.

"I'm going back to architecture. It will allow me the chance to do something that invigorates me, instead of drains me."

"I'm glad. You deserve to be happy."

"There's only one thing that would make me happier."

"What?"

"Come home with me. We're a good team. And I will be there for you this time if you'll give me that chance. I love you, Renee. Let me spend the rest of my life proving that."

"I love you, too. And there's nothing I'd like more than to spend the rest of our lives together."

* * * * *

Don't miss another sexy story from the men
at Maddox Communications with
BILLIONAIRE'S CONTRACT ENGAGEMENT,
available next month
from Silhouette Desire.

*Rancher Ramsey Westmoreland's temporary cook
is way too attractive for his liking.
Little does he know Chloe Burton came to his
ranch with another agenda entirely....*

That man across the street had to be, without a doubt, the most handsome man she'd ever seen.

Chloe Burton's pulse beat rhythmically as he stopped to talk to another man in front of a feed store. He was tall, dark and every inch of sexy—from his Stetson to the well-worn leather boots on his feet. And from the way his jeans and Western shirt fit his broad muscular shoulders, it was quite obvious he had everything it took to separate the men from the boys. The combination was enough to corrupt any woman's mind and had her weakening even from a distance. Her body felt flushed. It was hot. Unsettled.

Over the past year the only male who had gotten her time and attention had been the e-mail. That was simply pathetic, especially since now she was practically drooling simply at the sight of a man. Even his stance— both hands in his jeans pockets, legs braced apart, was a pose she would carry to her dreams.

And he was smiling, evidently enjoying the conversation being exchanged. He had dimples, incredibly sexy dimples in not one but both cheeks.

"What are you staring at, Clo?"

Chloe nearly jumped. She'd forgotten she had a lunch date. She glanced over the table at her best friend from college, Lucia Conyers.

"Take a look at that man across the street in the blue shirt, Lucia. Will he not be perfect for Denver's first issue of *Simply Irresistible* or what?" Chloe asked with so much excitement she almost couldn't stand it.

She was the owner of *Simply Irresistible*, a magazine for today's up-and-coming woman. Their once-a-year Irresistible Man cover, which highlighted a man the magazine felt deserved the honor, had increased sales enough for Chloe to open a Denver office.

When Lucia didn't say anything but kept staring, Chloe's smile widened. "Well?"

Lucia glanced across the booth at her. "Since you asked, I'll tell you what I see. One of the Westmorelands—Ramsey Westmoreland. And yes, he'd be perfect for the cover, but he won't do it."

Chloe raised a brow. "He'd get paid for his services, of course."

Lucia laughed and shook her head. "Getting paid won't be the issue, Clo—Ramsey is one of the wealthiest sheep ranchers in this part of Colorado. But everyone knows what a private person he is. Trust me—he won't do it."

Chloe couldn't help but smile. The man was the epitome of what she was looking for in a magazine cover and she was determined that whatever it took, he would be it.

"Umm, I don't like that look on your face, Chloe. I've seen it before and know exactly what it means."

She watched as Ramsey Westmoreland entered the store with a swagger that made her almost breathless. She *would* be seeing him again.

Look for Silhouette Desire's
HOT WESTMORELAND NIGHTS
by Brenda Jackson,
available March 9
wherever books are sold.

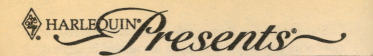

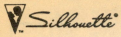

ROMANTIC
SUSPENSE

Sparked by Danger, Fueled by Passion.

Introducing a brand-new miniseries
Lawmen of Black Rock

Peyton Wilkerson's life shatters when her
four-month-old daughter, Lilly, vanishes.
But handsome sheriff Tom Grayson is
determined to put the pieces together and
reunite her with her baby. Will Tom be able
to protect Peyton and Lilly while fighting
his own growing feelings?

Find out in
His Case, Her Baby
by
CARLA CASSIDY

Available in March wherever books are sold

REQUEST YOUR FREE BOOKS!

2 FREE NOVELS
PLUS 2
FREE GIFTS!

Silhouette®

Desire®

Passionate, Powerful, Provocative!

YES! Please send me 2 FREE Silhouette Desire® novels and my 2 FREE gifts (gifts are worth about $10). After receiving them, if I don't wish to receive any more books, I can return the shipping statement marked "cancel." If I don't cancel, I will receive 6 brand-new novels every month and be billed just $4.05 per book in the U.S. or $4.74 per book in Canada. That's a saving of almost 15% off the cover price! It's quite a bargain! Shipping and handling is just 50¢ per book in the U.S. and 75¢ per book in Canada.* I understand that accepting the 2 free books and gifts places me under no obligation to buy anything. I can always return a shipment and cancel at any time. Even if I never buy another book, the two free books and gifts are mine to keep forever.

225 SDN E39X 326 SDN E4AA

Name	(PLEASE PRINT)	

Address		Apt. #

City	State/Prov.	Zip/Postal Code

Signature (if under 18, a parent or guardian must sign)

Mail to the **Silhouette Reader Service:**
IN U.S.A.: P.O. Box 1867, Buffalo, NY 14240-1867
IN CANADA: P.O. Box 609, Fort Erie, Ontario L2A 5X3

Not valid for current subscribers to Silhouette Desire books.

Want to try two free books from another line?
Call 1-800-873-8635 or visit www.morefreebooks.com.

* Terms and prices subject to change without notice. Prices do not include applicable taxes. N.Y. residents add applicable sales tax. Canadian residents will be charged applicable provincial taxes and GST. Offer not valid in Quebec. This offer is limited to one order per household. All orders subject to approval. Credit or debit balances in a customer's account(s) may be offset by any other outstanding balance owed by or to the customer. Please allow 4 to 6 weeks for delivery. Offer available while quantities last.

Your Privacy: Silhouette Books is committed to protecting your privacy. Our Privacy Policy is available online at www.eHarlequin.com or upon request from the Reader Service. From time to time we make our lists of customers available to reputable third parties who may have a product or service of interest to you. If you would prefer we not share your name and address, please check here. ☐

Help us get it right—We strive for accurate, respectful and relevant communications. To clarify or modify your communication preferences, visit us at www.ReaderService.com/consumerschoice.

SDES10

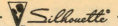

SPECIAL EDITION

FROM *USA TODAY* BESTSELLING AUTHOR
CHRISTINE RIMMER

BRAVO FAMILY TIES

A BRIDE FOR JERICHO BRAVO

Marnie Jones had long ago buried her wild-child impulses and opted to be "safe," romantically speaking. But one look at born rebel Jericho Bravo and she began to wonder if her thrill-seeking side was about to be revived. Because if ever there was a man worth taking a chance on, there he was, right within her grasp....

Available in March
wherever books are sold.

Two families torn apart by secrets and desire
are about to be reunited in

a sexy new duet by

Kelly Hunter

EXPOSED: MISBEHAVING WITH THE MAGNATE

#2905 Available March 2010

Gabriella Alexander returns to the French vineyard she
was banished from after being caught in flagrante with the
owner's son Lucien Duvalier—only to finish what they started!

REVEALED: A PRINCE AND A PREGNANCY

#2913 Available April 2010

Simone Duvalier wants Rafael Alexander and always has, but
they both get more than they bargained for when a night of
passion and a royal revelation rock their world!

www.eHarlequin.com

HP12905

THE WESTMORELANDS

NEW YORK TIMES
bestselling author

BRENDA JACKSON

HOT WESTMORELAND NIGHTS

Ramsey Westmoreland knew better than to lust after the hired help. But Chloe, the new cook, was just so delectable. Though their affair was growing steamier, Chloe's motives became suspicious. And when he learned Chloe was carrying his child this Westmoreland Rancher had to choose between pride or duty.

Available March 2010 wherever books are sold.

Always Powerful, Passionate and Provocative.

Visit Silhouette Books at www.eHarlequin.com

SD73013